THE ASHEN ORB BOUNTY

PATRICK DUGAN

To my best friend Mike, whose love of games brought me into worlds I never knew existed. He passed way too soon, but his memory will live on. RIP my friend.

Michael A. Mahady
1966-2023

The vultures pecked at the corpses where they lay after an attempted ambush. Kobold blood and gore pooled on the stone road from the fight. Saria and her team, on the way back to Moonbourne after a bounty mission, had stumbled across the kobolds looting the dead members of the ambushed caravan. Saria had thought the kobolds had attacked the caravan, but her troop had dispatched them so easily that now she wondered.

Two parked wagons stood in the weeds off to the side of the path. The remains of the unfortunate gnome merchant and her guards weren't any prettier to look at than the deceased kobolds. The hand-pulled carts sat empty, which led Saria to suspect the kobolds had happened across the dead and not that they had attacked the merchant. Why the dirty little scavengers hadn't run when the Blades arrived confused her even more. At least the kobolds wouldn't bother any more travelers.

"Fucking kobold rats," Saria mumbled. She wiped the entrails from her sword on a torn piece of cloth from the back of the wagon. One of the dead guards was a huge orc.

There was no way a bunch of dirt rats could best him. The guards must have been dead, and the kobolds did what they did best, scavenge. In fact, kobolds were barely more sentient than sewer rats. While they wore clothing, carried crude weapons, and had a language of sorts, they tended to live in sewers or other locales that allowed them to scavenge for food and other necessities. They survived on the remains of the larger monsters and were cowards in Saria's experience.

It had to be that something else killed the merchant and her guards, and the red-skinned rats were just feasting off the remains. Whatever creature it was, that something was long gone. Their ranger, Olive, hadn't indicated tracks of a larger monster or any other signs of a mass attack, and she was one of the few people Saria trusted completely.

The five members of the Shadow Blades moved around the ambush site. Ayre went through the pouches and packs of the deceased looking for anything of value. Why bother? The merchant's packs were gone, the bodies already looted, by the kobolds or whoever had been here before them.

That being said, Saria learned long ago not to waste her breath on telling Ayre not to "just have one more look-see" for valuables. She had to admit, at times he'd found a few trinkets that had brought in some coin, so maybe she was wrong. Either way, she wasn't about to join in the ghoulish search.

Olive, a small smile on her face, sat with her back against a tree. She carefully cleaned and replaced each of her used arrows into her quiver. The dryad's green tinged skin allowed her to creep through the forest without being seen, which was a great advantage in the wilds.

Perric knelt in a spot free of blood and gore with his winged sword in front of him. The big man's eyes were closed, and his lips moved in silent prayer. A kobold had gotten a lucky strike and had gashed Perric's arm. The wound stopped bleeding and closed as the paladin prayed to Drohara, the goddess of the sun.

Over the last couple of years, Saria, Perric, Ayre, and Olive had learned to fight together and made a bit of coin as well. The bounties they completed helped the towns and other folk stave off the infestation of monsters that roamed the continent of Southern Holm. With two fighters, a thief, and a ranger, they needed magic to bolster their troop.

Right now, that was Jileli, the newest of the Blades, who had joined the troop eight days ago in Whitecrest while they were searching for a new mage. Saria was pleased so far. The small, slight woman had handled herself well in her first action with the troop. The blood mage had been shunned by a lot of other teams that found her magic profane and didn't like the fact she had horns and long purple hair, gifts from her succubus side. While she'd never worked with a half-demon before, Saria didn't care if she had tentacles and sang off-key. If her magic could keep her team alive and fighting, that was all that mattered. Perric had argued loudly against adding her, but after the troll bounty, whose head now resided in a bag next to Perric, had killed Hilo, their previous mage, they needed her.

The troll bounty had gone to plan if you didn't count Hilo's death. Whitecrest had been close enough to hire on the blood mage. Now they were returning to Moonbourne to get paid and attend the troop faire to find a new bounty. The kobolds had been an unexpected delay, though a short one.

Perric pulled his sword free of the ground and sheathed it. Olive slung her bow over her back, while Ayre and Jileli joined Saria. The Blades weren't nearly as strong as most of the troops, but they had gained a reputation for getting results. One day, they might be experienced enough to venture into the Wildlands or Dragon's Reach, but that was a long way off.

"Olive, take point," Saria said.

"Got it," Olive said with a wink. The green-skinned dryad set off at a good clip. Perric moved just behind her with Jileli and Ayre next and Saria bringing up the rear. The "road" they followed from Whitecrest to Moonbourne had been overgrown since the Eylnian Empire fell one hundred and twenty years ago. Now the monsters outnumbered the people who lived in Southern Holm. That was bad for the people, but the good part was the coin to be made in eliminating the worst of the trash.

Saria now second guessed her decision to take the overland path. The river took less time, but with marauders and river monsters frequently sacking boats between Whitecrest and Auano and all the towns along the Marrimon River, it was more dangerous.

Perric slowed until Saria came up next to the big man. He glanced at her with a familiar mulish glint in his eyes.

"I'm not changing my mind," Saria said before the paladin could launch into his newest list of reasons why Jileli shouldn't be a part of the Blades. Perric had an eye for the ladies, but he drew the line at half elven succubi with "unholy" magic. Was it the half succubus that was the issue, or the blood magic? It must be the magic, because Perric wasn't exactly picky about the women he bedded.

"Saria, I am a holy paladin, and she is an abomination. What is to say she won't gut us and use our blood for unholy rituals?"

Saria laughed.

Perric's face went solid red. "It's not funny. She is dangerous."

She stopped and turned to face him, looking him straight in the eye, which was easy to do because she was nearly his height. She adjusted her scabbard while she collected her thoughts. "We are all dangerous, or we'd be hiding behind the walls like the people we protect. Anyone, and I mean anyone, who is brave enough to fight at our side is worth the risk."

"Hilo was a much more accomplished mage." Perric's face still showed his troubled feelings. It was a good thing he enjoyed the whorehouse more than the gambling dens, because every emotion showed on his face as soon as he had it.

"Hilo threw a fireball into a cave and almost killed us all," Saria said. The fire mage had been erratic to the point of being more dangerous than the monsters they fought. Not that she'd wanted him dead but calling him an accomplished mage was a stretch at the best of times.

"Well, it got the troll out of his lair."

"We were lucky. That troll was a cub. If mama troll had happened on us, we'd be dinner."

"Speaking of dinner," Ayre said from where the other three had stopped. He gestured at a small clearing. "This is a good place to camp for the night, or do you two want to keep arguing until we attract every monster in the surrounding woods?"

Saria hadn't realized they were speaking loud enough to be heard, but elves had much better hearing than she and Perric possessed. Anyone else would have ignored it, but not Ayre with his caustic wit and over the top sense of humor.

"Make camp. We'll continue on to Moonbourne in the morning," Saria said. How good was Jileli's hearing? As good as Ayre's? Perric was a good fighter and better friend, but he had blind spots a Yeti could walk through. He didn't have to shower her with flowers and welcomes, but she couldn't let his rudeness drive away a potentially valuable team member.

Hopefully, the rest of the journey would be uneventful. Saria shrugged. It could happen.

2

The sun crested over the world as the Blades resumed their trek to Moonbourne the next morning. Olive had returned from scouting to lead them along the broken road.

"There is something going on up ahead," Olive said. She pointed back the way she'd come. "There are footprints, probably some of the survivors from the caravan fled this way, but either they were dragging something or the did a horrible job at covering their tracks."

In the distance, smoke billowed, carrying an awful stench. It drifted through the trees weaving around the trunks and limbs. The normal forest noises of birds and other wildlife went still.

"It could be a forest fire," Perric said with a sniff.

"Could be," Saria said. The smell contained an odor she couldn't quite place. "We should check it out."

"We'll be late for the troop faire," Ayre said with a smirk. "I'm sure the mistress won't mind."

"It shouldn't take us too far out of the way." Olive paced

back and forth, a frown marring her smooth brow. "If it is a fire we need to know. The trees must be protected."

"A dryad and her trees," Perric said with a grin. "Very well, I say we check it out. Olive won't rest until we know."

Saria glanced at Jileli. The newest addition didn't say much, but what little they'd seen of she hoped she'd be a good fit. "Jileli?"

"I'll go along with the Blades," she said after a moment's pause. "I've never been to the troop faire before."

Ayre linked his arm through hers. "Then we should be off. Who are we to stand in the way of Jileli's first time at the troop faire? The sooner we find the fire, the sooner Perric can start bedding all the whores in Moonbourne."

"Now listen here, Ayre," Perric said. The big man's cheeks flushed red. "I don't bed them all, I am selective."

Ayre winked at the blood mage. "What he means is he can't afford them all."

Saria stepped between the two of them. "You two are worse than goblin brothers. Olive, take the lead. Perric, bring up the rear."

Ayre flashed a wicked grin. "According to my sources, Perric is a fan of—"

"Enough!" Saria said. In the quiet of the forest, her words were much louder than normal.

Olive set off with Ayre and Jileli behind her. Saria stayed between the front and the grumbling Perric. Saria studied Jileli and Ayre as they walked together. Most elves didn't have horns or purple hair, but that was the only difference between the blood mage and other elves she had seen. So far. She appreciated Ayre taking her under his wing, but she noticed Jileli didn't say a lot, which was common when the thief was on a roll.

Perric moved up to walk beside Saria. "One of these days his mouth is going to get him killed."

"I don't know why you let him bug you. He whores, gambles, and drinks. At least you only have one vice." Well, two if you counted the holier than thou routine, but she let that slide. Perric and Ayre had been the first two who joined Saria after her previous troop had died in an ambush. They were as close to family as she had, along with Regina, the Mistress of Bounties in Moonbourne. She'd found Saria as a teenager on the streets of Whitecrest and had cleaned her up and taught her to fight. Armed with a purpose beyond scavenging in the alleys and gutters like a—a kobold. Except taller. Granted, she was taller than most humans, too, so that wasn't saying much.

Saria had signed on as one of the Duke's personal guards before she'd left to take up bounty hunting. Hiding behind stone walls had never sat well with her, not when innocent people were being killed by the roaming monsters.

"I don't know." Perric scratched at the growth on his chin. "I think it's—"

A small crack came from a group of shrubs off to the right.

Olive drew and loosed her arrow in one smooth motion. A shrill squeal erupted from the foliage. Perric ran to the spot and pulled out the body of a kobold. The arrow had taken him square in the chest.

"Nice shot, Olive," the paladin said with genuine admiration.

He pulled the arrow free, tossed it to Olive, and dropped the body to the ground. "Looks like the rats are trailing us."

"Why?" Saria asked. "We had no trouble eliminating twenty of them yesterday."

"Something's not quite right about it," Olive said. "Could they be trailing a larger monster and hoping to feed off the corpses?"

"That wouldn't be great for us." The smell of smoke intensified as the trail banked to the left. Saria gathered the Blades around her. "But if there is something that just killed a whole caravan of people, that's not good. Do we head to Moonbourne or keep on? We're two days from the faire."

"We are close." Olive fidgeted with the arrow Perric had tossed her.

"Scout first, act after. Perric, you take the right, I'll have the left. If things look bad, we run to Moonbourne and get the other troops to come help," Saria said, pulling her off-hand dirk out and readying her sword.

"Prepare yourselves to fight," Ayre said softly. "We are being watched."

Saria took the lead with Perric a step behind. Jileli stayed behind Saria while Olive and Ayre flanked the group. Sunlight filtered through the canopy above, gleaming on the trails of smoke. Trees crowded around a stone wall that appeared out of place. Outlines of old buildings were present in the forest. The sound of a single scream that ended abruptly reached them as they neared the tall stone walls and double iron gate that ringed what looked like a cemetery.

"This is the place," Jileli said, motes of magic sparkling around her fingers.

The massive black iron gates blocked the path to the cemetery beyond. Saria couldn't help wondering if they were the gates to hell.

3

The iron gates were skillfully wrought, but the ravages of time had corroded away many of the ornate features. A thick, rusted chain with an ancient padlock hung from the front. Blood coated a few of the spikes that jutted from the top of the wall where they hadn't broken off.

"Allow me," Ayre said, sheathing his daggers and producing an oilskin packet. He pulled out a wire pick and tried it in the lock. "Fucking post locks, so arcane."

"Can you open it?" Saria said and instantly regretted it. The thief's ego was only eclipsed by his skill. He'd been with the Brotherhood of Blood before a dragon had eaten most of the troop. He'd signed on with the Blades after a particularly rowdy bar brawl.

He looked offended in a way only an elf could. "Why, fearless leader, would you rather hack away at the chain? I can open a spring tensioned post lock with my eyes closed."

Saria nodded to him. "You are the master thief. I retract my question."

"Maybe Perric could bore it with his tales of his bedroom

prowess with the harlots of Whitecrest until it yawns and opens on its own?"

"No need to get nasty about it," Perric grumbled.

"Of course not," Ayre said with a mocking bow. "I'm sure your skill in the bed is second only to your tact."

Perric stiffened, but Saria placed her hand on the paladin's shoulder. "Ayre, just open the lock."

"As you command, my leader." Ayre considered a couple more picks before sliding one into the lock. Ever so gently, he twisted the tool until a grinding click announced the lock had opened. He removed the lock, tossing it into the brush. The chain followed suit.

"Excellent," Perric said, stepping forward, but Ayre put his hand on the Paladin's chest.

"Rush, rush, rush. No wonder you are sought after by the courtesans across Southern Holm. As you well know, a little lube goes a long way." Ayre produced a bottle of liquid that he sprayed on the hinges of the rusted gate. Red tinged bubbles burst forth from the metal, dripping down the gate. After a few moments, Ayre pushed the gate, and it swung open. The small amount of noise was covered by another scream.

"Nicely done," Saria said, keeping her hand on the hot headed Perric. She caught his eye and the big man shrugged. No fights today.

"What is that smell?" Jileli asked, holding her nose closed. "It is awful."

"Burnt meat," Perric said.

Saria strode into the cemetery. On each side stood large stone mausoleums. Any names inscribed on the plaques had long since been eroded away by the elements. A row of mismatched burial chambers functioned as a wall in front of them. To the left, a weed-choked opening led deeper into the cemetery.

"I don't like this place," Olive said from Saria's left flank. The volume of the smoke increased as they moved through the gloomy cemetery. Another mausoleum stood off to the left, covered in spidery vines that gave the illusion that the structure had cracked. Ahead sat a group of smaller structures. Most of them had collapsed to some degree.

Saria lengthened her stride as she plunged into the encroaching darkness. The sun was fully out, but the smoke kept its cleansing rays away. Confused bats flitted above in the gloom.

A large monument to a fallen god regarded them silently as they finally came upon a bonfire. Stone sarcophaguses ringed a clearing, with a massive bonfire in the middle. Assorted packs and weapons were strewn around the opening.

A troll, easily twice the size of the one they'd killed outside Whitecrest, stood over the dead body of a human. The troll had dark green skin that was covered in warts and other growths. Its hair hung past its shoulders in greasy clumps. Long fingers with wicked talons held a club that had pieces of metal cobbled on to it.

The body of the human victim seemed to have burst open, its insides splayed out like a macabre art piece. Kobolds feasted on the entrails, chittering loudly as they fought over the remains. Their red skin camouflaged the blood spatter from their grisly meal. An orc, badly injured but alive, lay on the ground. His eyes grew wide when he saw the Blades enter the clearing. "Help!"

The troll's head came up and it roared a challenge. The kobolds scattered at the sound. They retreated behind the tall, gangly troll.

"Oh, fuck," Ayre said.

He wasn't wrong.

4

Before the Blades could react, the troll hefted its
spiked club and jumped across the distance. The
club slammed down on Olive, sending a spray of
blood into the air. The dryad dropped like a sack of rocks.

"Olive!" Perric screamed. He slashed at the troll, but the
beast was far faster than expected. It dove to the side and
took a swipe at Saria. She turned the club aside with her
longsword and stabbed the troll with her dagger. It cut
through the skin on the troll's arm.

It leapt back, but Saria saw the wound begin to close.
Damn trolls healed at an alarming rate. Perric came in from
the left, but a group of kobolds charged him.

The troll advanced, using the club like a spear. Saria
ducked under one thrust and opened up a gash across the
troll's muscled chest. Blood dripped on his ragged leather
pants from the cut before it closed.

Ayre darted in from behind the troll and slashed across
the back of his legs, eliciting a loud roar of pain. More
kobolds charged, grabbing at Ayre and he spun to face the
new threat.

It was unusual for kobolds to attack, but they had the numbers and with the troll in the middle of the fight, they must have thought the Blades were easy pickings.

Saria spun, raking her sword across the troll's hip. It caught her with a backhanded strike, sending her tumbling. At the last second, she twisted so she didn't land in the hotly burning bonfire. The smoke coming off it was thick and acrid.

If Perric was right about the burnt meat, then the troll might have had a grisly dinner before they arrived.

The troll watched her get to her feet. Past the monster, Saria saw Olive laid out on the ground. Jileli had a dagger in one hand and stood behind a blue tinged shield that the kobolds threw themselves at to no effect. Ayre and Perric were killing kobolds, but for each one they slew another replaced it. The nest must be close by.

The troll roared a challenge and beat the club on the ground. Saria hoped the others would dispatch the vermin quickly, because the troll was an imposing opponent. She charged, her sword held high as if she intended to swing overhand. The troll took its club in both hands and swung directly down at Saria's head. She threw herself into a slide and went between the troll's legs. The club struck behind her. She opened up a good-sized rent that sprayed green blood like a waterfall. The troll shrieked.

"So, you can be hurt." Saria kicked the back of the troll's injured leg, sending it stumbling. It caught its balance and turned to face her. Its eyes blazed with fury. Saliva dripped off its long, needle-like teeth. And even as deeply as she'd sliced it, the leg wounds seemed to be closing already.

Saria surveyed the fight. Shit, since the woods weren't burning down, would they be better off grabbing Olive and running?

Two kobolds ran at Saria. She kicked the first and it flew

into the troll. The other she decapitated with a strike from her sword. "Come on, big boy. Let's dance."

The troll threw the kobold across the clearing and ran at her. Its club arced at her head, but she ducked and sliced at its knee. A flurry of blows were exchanged, neither getting the better of the other due to the troll's healing ability.

Saria kept landing hits and avoiding the club. She ducked under a clumsy swing and went for a killing blow, but her foot slipped in green troll blood. The club caught her on the shoulder. She flew toward the bonfire and thudded against a cast-off pack. The damage to her shoulder throbbed enough that it might interfere with lifting her sword.

With that arm, anyway.

The troll chortled. It set the hair on Saria's arm straight up. It lumbered over to her, the club ready to end her. At least it would be fast.

Perric charged in and slashed at the troll. It pulled back, just missing the blade that would have lopped its head off. The paladin recovered and blocked the club with his sword. He kicked out, slamming his booted foot into the troll's knee. It stumbled back.

Saria pulled herself to her feet. "Too bad that strike missed."

"It worked last time." Perric pulled the leather bag from his hip and threw it at the troll. It bounced across the ground, expelling the troll cub's head.

The troll let out a loud keening wail at the sight. Perric charged in while it was distracted and took a punch to the chest for his troubles. The beast leapt into the air, intent on landing on the warrior from above.

Perric managed to roll to safety, and the troll looked ready to jump again.

With a burst of speed, Saria ran and tackled the troll from the side, knocking him off balance. She threw herself out of its way and slammed into ground. The wind whooshed from her lungs.

Perric repositioned his grip on his sword with a growl that sounded a lot like a troll. "Saria, let's take him down."

The troll roared, its back to the fire. Saria, to one side of the monstrous beast, rolled behind the giant troll and got on hands and knees. Perric charged. At the last moment, he jumped and kicked the troll square in the chest.

Under normal circumstances, the troll might have kept his footing, but when he stepped back, he fell over Saria. With a shriek, he tumbled directly into the raging bonfire. Thick oily smoke billowed off the screaming troll. It thrashed, which just buried it deeper in the flames.

The smell became unbearable. Perric started retching as Saria stood and stumbled away.

That was when she saw Olive.

5

aria!" Jileli shouted, kneeling next to the downed ranger. "She's dying."

Saria skidded to a stop by the blood mage's side. "Perric. We need you."

The big man ran to Olive's prone form. He thrust his blade into the ground by the Dryad's head. "Drohara, I beseech you to grant me the power to save Olive's life."

Jileli held Olive's hand. A horrified look crept across the blood mage's face. "We're losing her."

Perric's hands glowed a soft golden color. He placed one hand on Olive's forehead and one at the base of her neck. Sparks flew and Perric reared back as jolts of power arced up his arms. Anger filled his words. "Jileli, let go of her. Are you trying to kill me?"

The startled woman dropped Olive's hand. "Save her."

Perric glowered and placed his hands back on the prone form of the ranger. The glow intensified, but no sparks flew this time. "Drohara, please help me save my friend."

The golden light swelled until Perric and Olive were completely encased in a translucent bubble of golden, pulsating energy. "Please, save this woman's life. She is a true warrior. We need her to continue to fight in your name."

The others watched in awe. Perric had healed them all in the past, except Jileli, but never had any of them been this close to death. The paladin's eyes were closed and his lips moved soundlessly.

Perric continued his prayers to his goddess. Magic scoured the dryad's body but slid away from her injuries. "I'm begging you, almighty Drohara. Please allow me to heal this woman."

Saria placed her hand on Perric shoulder as a sign of support. Sweat ran down the paladin's ashen face. She gripped his shoulder tighter, lending her support, willing him to heal Olive.

Suddenly a wave of vertigo swept over her. She closed her eyes, assuming the blow had been harder than she'd thought, but the second she did a vision flashed behind her eyes as vividly as real life. A woman dressed in a long, flowing white gown stood before Perric. His armor shone like the sun. Gone was the weariness Saria had been experiencing since the fight. The proud warrior of Drohara bowed before his goddess.

"I'm sorry, my child, but she is too far gone," a soft voice whispered. "She has moved too close to The Tranquil Gardens for me to interfere."

Drohara carried her traditional sun shield and spear. Her long copper hair hung to her waist. Perric fell to his knees in the vision.

"Perric, rise," Drohara said softly.

The holy knight stood to face his goddess. Fields of grass surround them as far as the eye could see. "My goddess, how may I serve you?"

Drohara studied him for a moment. A sadness crossed her face. "There is a great evil across the land. You travel in the shadow of the eternal and must do everything in your power to stop the encroaching darkness."

"How do I do that? Should I leave my troop for a holy quest?"

"No, you are where I mean for you to be. You will reach a crossroads where you will be forced to make a choice. Consider carefully, for the most certain path is often the most dangerous."

"What choice will I have to make?"

Drohara set her hand on Perric's bowed head. "My child, I know you, the struggles you've faced, the pain you have endured, and the fear that grips your soul. Follow your heart and it will guide you to the right path."

"I'm not worthy of your praise. I am broken."

She let out a small, warm laugh. "You are trying to be better, which is just as important as being whole. Just remember, what you believe is no more valid than the beliefs of the others you journey with. I accept all, not just those who believe as we do."

Perric nodded. "I will listen and obey."

She lifted his chin. Her piercing golden eyes seemed to take in everything but Saria. Or if she knew Saria was there, she didn't care.

"I don't want you to obey. I want you to think for yourself and follow me because you know it is the right thing to do."

"Yes, my lady Drohara," Perric said. "What of Olive? I don't want her to die."

"Death is but another step along the journey. She is beyond my help, but there are choices to be made if you want to save your friend."

The vision faded and Saria opened her eyes.

Perric pulled his hands back from Olive and bowed his head in shame. Tears ran down his face. "I'm sorry. She's beyond my skills to heal her."

Saria's head swam with what she'd witnessed. How could a goddess not be strong enough to return Olive to life? The realization hit her like a warhammer. She saw it in Perric's face as well. He'd blame himself for failing his friend though he'd done everything in his power to help. She decided that telling him he'd witnessed his spiritual communion would shame him even more, so she stayed quiet.

"She's not beyond mine," Jileli announced, scanning the cemetery.

"Anything," Saria said, desperate to save their ranger—and her friend. "What do you need?"

Jileli pointed at the whimpering orc guard laid where the troll had left him for a snack. "Bring him here."

Saria and Ayre ran to grab the wounded orc. Perric stepped between them and the fallen orc. "This is murder. I won't stand for it."

Jileli's eyes glowed a dark purple. "I'm not asking for permission. Move!"

Perric stepped to the side, retrieved his sword, and interceded again. "All life is sacred. This is demon magic."

"Perric, what is more important, your beliefs or Olive's life?" Mind made up, Saria pushed past the paladin and set the dying orc at the blood mage's feet. She suspected what a blood mage would have to do to attempt to heal such deadly wounds, and though Perric's methods were preferable, she'd take what she could get.

Ayre dropped the feet and turned on Perric. "Listen to Saria. He'll be dead in a few minutes anyhow. Let Jileli try to save our friend."

"Drohara told me there was another way to save Olive. I won't interfere." He lowered his sword, turned his back, and walked away.

"Thank you," Jileli said to the retreating Perric. "Stay back."

"Just save her," Ayre said, following Saria to join Perric, where he sat against the stone wall of a sarcophagus.

Saria had not truly experienced blood magic before taking Jileli on with the Blades. Saria felt a tingle race down her arms in anticipation at the same time as her guilt of sacrificing the orc raged in her conscious. Ayre was right, the orc would die from the massive wounds he'd suffered as would Olive if Jileli didn't save her.

"Thank you for your gift of life, my friend," Jileli said to the orc before she took the guard's head in her hands and started her spell. The mage's horns glowed with a deep purple color that Saria found beautiful and terrifying. The orc screamed, but the troll had broken his back, so there wasn't much he could do to stop the mage. Streaks of red trickled from the poor guard. Saria wanted to plug her ears, but again, a strange mixture of fear and longing came over her. She couldn't take her eyes off the casting.

She realized she wasn't just fascinated. She could actually hear the call of the blood magic. Part of her rejoiced in the raw power Jileli wielded. Her skin tingled like right before a lightning strike. The rest shuddered in horror that she was using another life to save Olive. Did the guard have a family that relied on him? Parents that would miss him? She told herself that even Perric couldn't heal the damage the guard had suffered, but she still warred with herself. Are we evil if we do this?

She shook her head to clear it, breaking the allure. Perric wasn't often right, but Jileli's magic came from demonic sources. Using it to help the Shadow Blades didn't change that fact.

The trickle of blood oozing from the orc became stronger as the spell continued. After a few moments, the orc thrashed for a moment and then went completely still. Jileli held a red globe the size of her hand. It pulsed with an unholy energy.

"That's disgusting." Perric spat on the ground to ward off evil. Old traditions would change nothing, but she stood by her decision. If it saved Olive, it was worth it.

"Quiet," Saria ordered. "It's beautiful in a twisted way." She stopped herself from reminding Perric his own goddess had literally just told him to respect other ways.

"If you like gruesome demonic rituals, I guess," Ayre said. "I'd rather be drinking at the Dragon's Nest than watching this."

"You've got that right." Perric pulled a cleaning cloth and a sharpening stone and set to work on his blade.

Saria just stared.

Jileli moved from the now dead orc to Olive's prone form. She placed the orb on the dryad's forehead. It sank like a boulder into quicksand. When the orb was gone, Jileli slumped to the ground.

"Will Olive live?" Saria asked, not sure if she wanted the answer.

"I don't know. She had traveled a good distance toward The Tranquil Gardens. She's got to want to come back," Perric said before stalking out of the clearing.

Olive picked this time to sit bolt upright. She screamed in terror. Her eyes flew around the clearing until they settled on Jileli. "What did you do to me?"

"She saved your life," Saria said, approaching the panicked dryad. "The troll nearly killed you."

The dryad's eyes were wide and her mouth worked, but no sound came out.

"The images will fade in a few moments," Jileli said weakly.

Ayre brought her a twig from his pack and handed it to her. The blood mage nodded her thanks before chewing on the olive branch.

"Don't know how you eat that stuff," Saria said, still holding Olive's hands. "Olive, you'll be fine."

"No. No, I won't. I need to heal properly."

Saria's head dropped. Olive being a dryad would need to commune with the trees and leave the Blades one short. She understood, but they were two days out from Moonbourne and could be attacked again. There was nothing she could do about it, but it stung. The Blades would continue on as they'd always done.

"Go, little sister, and commune with the grove," Ayre said, holding out his hand to her. She accepted it and got to her feet. Saria caught the dryad before she could fall. The three of them limped through the graveyard and out through the iron gates. Olive went to the giant oak where Perric stood waiting for them.

"I heard you calling me, Perric," Olive said. "I wanted to come back, but I couldn't see the path."

"I'm sorry, Olive. I tried my best to help you." Tears stood in the corner of his eyes.

"I know you did. It will take time, but the trees will nurture and restore me." She reached out and touched his face. "She was right about you. Listen to her."

"Who?" Perric asked, slightly confused.

"Drohara." Olive reached out and touched the oak tree. Her hand slid into the tough bark like it was water. Her body melded with the tree as she stepped into it. After a moment, she was gone.

Ayre shook his head slowly as they all stared at the oak tree where the dryad had disappeared. "Who else needs a drink?"

6

Perric removed his helm and ran a shaking hand over his brown hair. Tears ran down his cheeks.

Saria put her hand on his shoulder. "I'll miss Olive too, but she can heal for as long as it takes and then rejoin us when she's ready."

Perric turned to face her. "Just trying to understand what happened. Drohara came to me while I was attempting to heal her. I think Olive heard her speaking to me."

She studied Perric, wondering again if she should mention that she'd been with him, too, but decided against it. Perric had joined Saria when she started the Blades a few years ago. He was a braggart, a womanizer, and overly moral when it came to judging others, but he was dependable in a fight and honest. She knew he desperately needed to prove himself, but she didn't know if it was his goddess or himself that he needed to impress.

Finding out Saria had also witnessed his goddess guiding him would not help matters right now.

"We should get moving if we're going to make it to the faire on time. The first round is on the troll, or at least the entire merchant caravan it killed," Ayre said, turning his hand over to show the small pile of brass, copper, and silver coins he'd looted from the packs. When in the world had he found time to do that?

"I'm not sure which of you is worse," Perric said, though Saria could tell his heart wasn't in it. "You stealing from the dead or the mage sacrificing lives of the innocent."

Jileli spun on the paladin. "Olive would be dead if not for my magic. That was the first time I've ever taken a being's life force to fuel my spells. Do you think I wanted to do it? What would you have had me do, let her die? It was an emergency and your way failed."

Perric firmed his lips and stalked back toward the road out of town. "I'll meet you at the road."

The three remaining members of the troops stared at the retreating back of the holy knight. He glowed softly in the greyish light as the bonfire continued to fill the air with oily fumes. He turned the corner and vanished from view.

"Well," Ayre said with a sardonic smile. "I guess there is a first for everything. No preaching? No arguments? Maybe Mr. Holier Than Thou is mellowing."

"Something happened that we missed," Jileli said, tapping her finger on her chin. The blood mage did look paler than usual. "During the healing, he was talking, but I couldn't make out the words."

"Praying, I'm sure," Ayre said with a laugh. "Probably that Avilya will be working at The Velvet Pearl when we arrive."

"Enough," Saria said before Ayre got on a roll. The elf's sense of humor left a lot to be desired at times. Now was definitely one of them. They'd nearly lost Olive and Jileli sacrificed a life to save her. The best thing for all of them now was to move on.

"Perric is right. We've got two days to make it to Moonbourne."

Ayre swept a bow that any court dandy would have killed for. "We follow our fearless leader, my Lady Saria."

Saria and Jileli exchanged glances and laughed. "Let's go," Saria said. She set a brisk pace, with Jileli to the right and Ayre to the left. The path meandered away from the graveyard until they reached the dirt road they would follow. Perric sat on a stump, cleaning his blade. He glanced up, stood, and sheathed his sword on his back.

"We'll go until we reach the Yamier's hut and sleep there for the night. We'll have to push ourselves tomorrow to reach Moonbourne, but I don't want to chance any more run-ins with monsters or anyone else," Saria said. She could hear the exhaustion in her own voice.

"I agree." Jileli's shoulders slumped and her horns were dull and lifeless, if you discounted all the ornamentation and banding attached to them. Clearly blood mages grew just as weary from magic use as any other kind of mage.

"I'll take the lead," Perric said.

"Well, I guess that's settled," Ayre said with a grin. "I am so looking forward to a drink, a warm bed, and some decent food."

"I as well," Perric said.

"Aren't we all," Jileli agreed.

Perric glared at Jileli, turned and strode down the road without waiting to see if they followed.

Well, at least they agreed on something. If only he'd listened to Drohara.

The journey to the hut went well, with no sightings of kobolds, trolls, or anything else. Ayre cooked a simple meal and the three remaining Shadow Blades drifted off into an uneasy sleep.

In the morning, they doused the fire, cleaned up after themselves, and made ready. After the fall of the Eylnian Empire, a group of magi had created special, hidden huts scattered across the continent. The Mistress of Bounties gave each member of the various troops an amulet that allowed the lodgings to be found. Without the charm, you'd walk right past the place and never suspect it was there.

Perric led on, still not speaking after a full day. It was unlike the big man to dwell on anything for this long.

"You want to talk about it?" Saria asked.

At her words, Perric startled as if he'd forgotten he had companions on this journey. How he could tune them out when Ayre hadn't quit chattering the whole time, Saria had no idea. Perric shrugged. "Drohara spoke to me when I was trying to heal Olive. She said I'd have a choice to make, but nothing more."

In fact, the goddess had told him that she accepted all beings not just the ones who believed as they did, but Saria just whistled softly. "Not every day your goddess comes to chat."

"It's only the second time she's done it since I took up her mantle. I don't know how or when this choice will come. What if I have to choose between saving one of you or leaving the Blades?"

She still didn't know how she'd been a part of Perric's vision, and it had to be one of his two dates with his goddess. Now she could never admit she'd been present as he spoke to her.

"No sense borrowing trouble," she said instead. Perric could be an ass, but she rarely saw this side of him. He was a broken man that wanted to serve the Goddess of the Sun.

"Easy for you to say," he grumbled.

"Yes, it is," Saria said, nudging her friend with her elbow. At least it got a grin. "I know how hard it is to put things

27

away. Hell, I don't even know who I am, let alone where I belong." Saria recalled the days of her being an orphan on the streets of Whitecrest. If Regina hadn't caught her trying to steal from her and put her to work, she'd probably be dead. "That's part of the reason I started the Blades. I've never had a family until we all started working together. One day, I'll know who I am meant to become. At some point, you'll know what decision you need to make. I'll support you no matter what."

"What if the choice is to kill you? Or Jileli? Or Ayre?"

"First off," Ayre said, catching up to the leaders. "You'd have to catch me, which in that scale mail of yours, you'll never do. With the others you might have a decent chance."

Perric's face reddened. "This is a private conversation."

The elf put a hand to his chest and gasped. "It is? Here I thought you were shooting the breeze while we made our way to Moonbourne. You might want to warn us when you are having a private talk."

"Leave it alone, Ayre," Jileli said, pushing his shoulder. "We've all paid our dues over the years. Perric has every right to his privacy."

"Thank you, Jileli," Perric said, though he didn't sound pleased about it. Jileli's personality was quiet and thoughtful, and normally Perric would have been friendly with her. He wasn't a prickly person who argued with all and sundry. But because of her half-demon side or her blood magic, Saria wasn't sure which was the issue, Perric's attitude toward her ensured the mage and paladin were oil and water.

"Less talking, more walking," Saria said. "We are out of the woods, so we are in the last stretch."

Saria took the lead, letting her long legs set the pace. This close to Moonbourne, one of Southern Holm's smaller walled cities, small farms dotted the landscape, and the road became more distinct due to frequent use. Farmers gave the troop a wave, but kept their bows and knives within easy reach. You didn't work the land and not take precautions. They'd done bounties for a half dozen farms around this area.

The sun was low in the sky when they crested the hill and spotted Moonbourne in the distance. They had finally arrived.

Saria wondered what waited for them on the other side of the walls.

7

Of all the cities in Southern Holm she'd visited, Moonbourne was Saria's favorite. The town rose to fame when the troop faire had been established to help protect the people of Southern Holm. Now that the walls were in sight, the road changed from hard packed dirt to cobblestones. The Blades made their way to the main entrance, where the massive oak and steel gate was open.

"At least they haven't closed up for the night," Ayre said. "My tender feet can't take walking to the other side of the town to gain entry."

"If you spent less time talking and more time fighting, you might have more stamina," Perric said.

Jileli laughed. "I don't care as long as there is a tub in my near future. I stink of kobold."

"Yeah, you do, but I was kind and didn't bring it up," Ayre said with a quick bow in the blood mage's direction.

"Seriously, that's all you've talked about for the past day," Perric said. "How bad everyone smells."

Ayre sniffed. "I haven't mentioned it recently."

Saria smiled. A bantering group was a cheerful group. These were the people closest to her, and she well knew that when things got tense, the claws and sharpened tongues came out. She keenly felt the hole Olive's loss had made in the group. The ranger was quiet and unassuming, but was the voice of reason for the Blades. The Dryad would heal fully, but she wondered if Olive would ever rejoin the Blades.

She and Perric, with their shorter human lifespans, might be dead and gone when Olive emerged from that oak tree.

The line to get into Moonbourne was short, with two guards checking carts of the merchants bringing their wares to market. After a few minutes, they reached the two guards who manned the gate. One was a tall elven woman with leather armor and a beautiful recurve bow on her back. The other was a stout dwarf leaning on his battle axe.

Ayre stepped forward, and Saria groaned.

"Mighty guardians of Moonbourne, you have the privilege of allowing the Shadow Blades entry into your fine city," Ayre said with his normal carnival barker shtick. "We await your approval before entering through the immaculate gates."

The elf looked at Saria. "Is he for real?"

"Unfortunately," Saria replied. "He thinks he's far more funny than he is."

"What!" Ayre announced in surprise. "I am Ayre, third in line for the eldar throne. Her majesty has set me on a quest to rid Southern Holm of the monsters and evil that have taken over since the fall of the Eylnian Empire."

"You elves talk a lot, but don't say nothin'," the dwarf said in a surly tone.

"You got that right," Perric and Jileli said at the same time.

Ayre passed out hurt looks to all involved. "We are off to the Dragon's Nest to grasp our destinies in both hands while we save the good people of Moonbourne."

"More like you be lookin' fer gold," the dwarf said. "Town is full up of troops. You'd be better off sleeping in the fields."

"How dare you suggest that I, Lord Ayre…"

A voice came from beyond the gate. "What is the holdup, Bariseal?"

"Nothing, Trollslayer," the shorter guard responded, but his darting eyes gave away his uneasiness.

The largest man Saria had ever met strode out through the gate. He was easily eight feet tall, bald, and covered with runic tattoos. Saria had known Trollslayer for years, and she still wasn't sure if she trusted the leader of the Moonbourne guard. The fact he controlled eldritch powers added to her discomfort.

People said things about folks who controlled eldritch powers. But they also said things about blood mages, and Jileli was turning out to be a boon companion.

"Trollslayer," Saria said with a nod to the big man.

"Saria!" He enveloped her in a bear hug, and the world disappeared for a moment. His colossal arms blocked off her sight, but not her breathing, and she could admit, having Trollslayer as a friend had its benefits. He set her back on the ground as gently as if she were a newborn kitten. "I expected you a couple of days ago."

She shrugged. "We ran into a few problems in the wilds. We have an open slot now if you'd want to join us."

The giant laughed, striking his gut. "Bounties are a young person's game. I'm too out of shape to be chasing about with you."

The truth was nowhere to be seen in that statement. Trollslayer had muscles on top of muscles. He could easily destroy an entire town without breaking a sweat. What he wasn't saying was that the Blades were too low on the boards for him to waste his time with.

"Offer is always open," Saria said.

He nodded. "Maybe one day I'll get bored and wander off on an adventure with you, but for now, the troop faire starts tomorrow. The Mistress told me she has a lot of new bounties on the board."

Perric hefted the burlap bag that contained the baby troll's head for their bounty. "That's good. We have a delivery to make as well."

"Then you better get to it," Trollslayer said, stepping aside to let the troop enter. He snagged Saria's arm as she passed. "Gnedain and the Skull Posse are in town."

"Fuck," Saria said. Gnedain, half-orc and all asshole, led the Skull Posse. They were more experienced than the Blades, and he never let Saria forget it. If the Blades took a bounty, more times than not, the Skulls tried to steal it. "Might as well get it over with."

Trollslayer laughed. "Call me if you need a hand. I hate that bastard."

"Don't we all," Saria said.

Once inside the stone walls, Moonbourne was laid out like a wagon wheel. All the streets went straight to the center of town where the duke and his family lived. Saria avoided the center like the plague. Royalty never paid well, if at all. Was better to work for the town guard, like Trollslayer, if one had to be a guard instead of a mercenary.

They followed the road to the Dragon's Nest on the southwestern spoke of the wheel of Moonbourne. The inn was three stories, with a large stable behind it, and more importantly, it connected to the troop faire. The stables were empty. Horses had been rare for longer than Saria had been alive since they attracted monsters. Merchants hired armed porters to pull wagons instead of chancing pack animals outside the city walls.

Perric entered the inn first, with the rest in tow. Rows of tables, mostly empty at this time of day, were scattered around the front room. An enormous fireplace stood at the far end. The wooden bar ran for well over fifty feet. Emme Maggot walked behind the bar. The halfling's eyes went wide as she spotted the Blades. If there was a warning to come, she never got to give it.

"Look, boys," Gnedain said from his bar stool. He jumped down. The half-orc, who was more broad than tall, strode across to confront Saria who towered over the shorter man. He reeked of stale ale and pipe smoke. He wore a silver skull pin on his chest, as did the rest of his troop. His armor hadn't been cleaned in a long time, if ever, and his stench put their kobold smell to shame. "The cleanup crew is here. Must be there are rats in the cellar that need to be taken care of."

A sibilant laugh came from Gnedain's right-hand man, Triz. The troglodyte stood six feet and carried a wooden staff. Rumor was he was a potent spell caster, but the Blades didn't work with butchers like the Skulls, who had a reputation for a lot of collateral damage and underhanded dealings. Gnedain tossed a brass coin to Perric, which hit his armor and bounced to the floor.

"Pick it up, grunt," Gnedain said to the knight.

Perric glowered. Triz took a step back. The Blades might not be top tier, yet, but they had a reputation for being smart and tough. The Skull Posse wasn't so far above them that they could guarantee the outcome of a fight.

The other three members of the Skulls formed up behind their leader, and Saria sensed Jileli and Ayre behind her doing the same. Troops blew off steam and caroused at the Faire. Gnedain had been looking to settle the score ever since the Blades had killed an ogre the Skulls had been tracking outside Whitecrest a year ago. Gnedain thought since they had roused the ogre into the Blades' path that they had the right to the coin. Saria offered to split the bounty and negotiations had gone downhill from there.

Gnedain pulled a dirk from his belt and stabbed at Saria. She blocked the attack with her mailed forearm and punched him square in the face. Greenish blood flew from his broken nose.

Perric drove a fist into Triz's abdomen, stopping the lizard-man from casting. He slumped forward from the force of the blow. Ayre slid past the downed mage and brandished two daggers before the three other Skulls. They pulled weapons, but when red hued blood magic from Jileli circled the Skulls, they froze.

"What is going on here?" a loud feminine voice rang from the end of the bar. "There is no fighting in my inn."

Regina Kirby, better known as the Mistress of Bounties, had arrived.

8

Saria, Gnedain, you both know better. The troop faire, and more importantly, the Dragon's Nest, is a safe zone. No fighting! You want to spill blood, get your next bounty, and do something productive."

"Yes, Regina," Saria said. The Mistress of Bounties was an attractive woman of middle years with shoulder length blond hair and a scar down her left cheek. She'd been a fierce warrior and the personal protector of the Duke of White-crest before his assassination. Regina had almost died trying to save the duke, but that hadn't been enough for the duke's family. With the population decimated, the cities and towns had guards or small armies to protect their immediate hold-ings, but that left most of the continent in the hands of the monsters. Regina took over the troop faire to help the people of Southern Holm fight against the monsters that poured through the nexus portals to the north and destroyed the Eylnian Empire. They had been open since the war began, allowing monsters to invade the continent. Behind her stood Selwyn, the Keeper of the Roles.

"Call her Mistress," Selwyn, said, his face flushing red.

The human stood around five eight and had arms the size of ale barrels. He'd been a mage with one of the top troops in his day, even killing a bronze dragon before injuries took their toll. Now, he tracked the bounties, did the payouts, and enforced Regina's rules. Saria knew he always had ulterior motives and didn't trust him as far as she could throw him. The Mistress didn't agree with her appraisal.

Regina waved him off. "Saria is allowed. I've known her since she was young."

"But Regina…" Gnedain started.

"You refer to me as Mistress or I'll slice out your tongue. Understood?"

Gnedain nodded. "Yes, Mistress."

"Get out of my sight or the Skulls will be exiled from the faire."

"Yes, Mistress." Gnedain cast a hateful glare at Saria. "We'll be here for the bidding."

"Fine," the Mistress said. "Now get out."

No one said a word as the Skull Posse leader pushed his troop out of the Dragon's Nest. None of the Blades understood why the Skull Posse had taken such a violent dislike of their troop over a single bounty, but little men like Gnedain needed few excuses for petty grievances.

Saria cracked her knuckles "We'll need to watch our backs while we are here."

"From that trash?" Ayre said with a laugh. "They can't even protect their pouches."

"What do you mean?" Perric asked.

Ayre produced four leather pouches and tossed one to each of the Blades. "I thought Gnedain's crew should pay a fine for breaking the peace."

"Oh, they will be furious," Jileli said, hefting the bag of coins.

Perric bounced the coin purse in his hand before holding

it out to Ayre. "This is stealing."

Ayre pushed the paladin's hand away. "Or it is a very nice evening at The Velvet Pearl with Avilya."

After considering, Perric handed back the pouch. "You enjoy it. I'll take care of my own fun."

"Have it your way," Ayre said with a smirk. "Shall we? The lads and ladies at the Velvet Pearl will be lonely if we don't arrive to entertain them."

"I think we should. It would be a shame to waste our time in Moonbourne and not see the lovely ladies at the Pearl," Perric said.

"What about you, Jileli?" Ayre asked. "Do you want to tag along and keep Perric out of trouble?"

Perric scowled and Jileli gave a brief smile. "Thank you, but no. I have other business to attend to."

"Keep your eyes open. The Skulls have a score to settle," Saria said.

"If they come after me again, I can take care of them," Jileli said. She stepped away, then looked back. "With your permission, of course."

Saria laughed. What sort of things would a half succubus do to take care of another troop? "You probably shouldn't kill them, if you can manage it."

Jileli favored her with another shy smile. "Of course. Though a lizard-man's blood would be valuable to me."

On second thought, she probably didn't want to know how the mage would handle the Skulls. Jileli's power was awe-inspiring, and so far she was as unassuming as Olive, but none of them knew a lot about the mage's abilities or her personal preferences.

"Where is Olive?" the Mistress asked after the others left.

"Healing," Saria responded, pulling a face. "We ran into a troll who was eating a caravan of merchant guards a day or so out from here."

"Really?" Selwyn whistled. "Trolls are tough. Must have been a nasty fight."

"Well, I'm sure Olive will be fine. Dryads are stronger than people give them credit for," Regina said. "Let's talk in private."

Emme trotted over and slid a mug of ale across the counter to Saria. "You'll want this."

Saria went to the bar, scooped up the mug and dropped a silver piece on the bar. "Thanks, Emme."

The halfling made the coin disappear and went off to greet a couple of gnomes that entered. Her boots thumped across the runway that had been built to allow the diminutive halfling to serve patrons. Talk about an ingenious way to compensate for her size. The gnomes hollered to the barkeep in their native tongue, and Emme responded in kind.

Saria followed Regina and Selwyn past the bar and the kitchen. They reached the Mistress' office door and Selwyn held it open for them, then entered before he closed it firmly behind them. The room was large, with a massive wooden desk taking up the center. The walls were lined with built-in bookcases, which held a lifetime of loot from a lifetime of adventuring. Saria glanced around the room, noticing the additions to the array of pendants, weapons, artifacts, and a few skulls that were new to the space.

The Keeper of the Roles mumbled a few words, and the runes etched into the walls and door glowed blue for an instant.

"No one can hear us," Selwyn announced.

"Thank you," Regina said, gesturing to an open chair facing the desk.

Saria took her seat while Selwyn propped himself in the corner where he faced Saria and the door. You didn't live long hunting bounties if you weren't cautious.

"All I can say is you are lucky to have survived that

encounter," Selwyn said. The Keeper had hands rested on his hips. They never strayed far from the daggers in his belt. He might have been a mage, but he was built like a barbarian.

The Mistress of Bounties grabbed three glasses and poured amber colored whiskey into each. She handed one to Saria, one to Selwyn, and took a large swig from hers before returning to her seat. "Chaos Clan went after a necromancer named Calrur three months ago, and we've not heard from them. Their bounty is still active, but no one has found it."

"I searched the aether for signs of the pendant and came up empty," Selwyn said. He took a swig from his glass. "Every bounty imprints the troop amulet when they accept it. All I can think is Chaos Clan failed."

This was news to Saria. The Blades had taken on many bounties, but being magically bound to the amulets that represented their official bounties explained a lot of things. It made sense that the Mistress would need to ensure the bounty was complete before it was paid out. Leave it to Selwyn to use magic to make coin.

But why were they telling her this, giving her this inside information? Saria took a sip, and the soothing heat flowed down her throat. "Have you sent another troop after it?"

Selwyn chuckled. "Always right to the heart of the matter."

Regina downed the rest of her whiskey and got a refill. Saria had never seen the Mistress of Bounties so tense, though worried summed it up better. She twirled the whiskey in her glass before she finished it in a single go. "I wanted to talk to you in private anyhow. I have a special bounty I need you to collect," Regina said.

Saria's heart went cold. Regina never played favorites, not even for her own son. Giving three special things to Saria in a row—information, the good whiskey, and this bounty—didn't bode well.

egina smiled. "Not to worry, I want you to take a
bounty. It is a special request by a mutual friend,
but I have to put it up for grabs. The other troops
will jump at this one, but I know where the item is located,
and they don't. If you move quickly, you'll make some easy
gold."

Growing up an orphan had instilled a large degree of
skepticism in Saria. No one gave gold away for free.
Anything that seemed too good to be true usually was. Saria
had known Regina for a good portion of her life. First while
she was with Duke Nalan's guards and then when she
became the Mistress of Bounties. Still, the whole thing felt
off. "Why us?"

"You do realize what an honor it is to be asked to take a
bounty?" Selwyn asked, ire sharpening his words. As far as
Saria could tell, the mage thought the sun rose and fell at the
Mistress' whims.

Regina laughed. "Selwyn, she has every right to ask.
Era'tal knows I would." Regina took another swallow from

her cup, and when Selwyn refilled it for her, she winked at him. "Do you remember Brar Opalback?"

Brar had been the sorceress for the duke. A dwarf from Ironhold, she stood around four feet tall and had the thick hair and dark coloring of her people with a well-earned reputation for being vindictive and occasionally cruel. "I do. That doesn't explain why you are handing it to the Blades."

"I'm giving it to you, not your troop. She's called in a favor and, frankly, you are the only one I trust to carry it out. You impressed Brar during our time working for Duke Nalan. She's located a magical artifact that was thought to have been destroyed during the fall of the Eylnian Empire. I know you will actually deliver the artifact."

Now it made sense. Most of the artifacts from the old empire had been lost in the monster wars or hidden away in the large strongholds. The few that remained were highly coveted and fetched far more gold than bounties ever would, assuming you weren't murdered for said item after you got your hands on it. "What does it do?"

Regina shrugged. "I don't get paid to ask questions and neither do you. She called it the ashen orb, but it could light campfires for all I know. The bounty will be listed as a stolen dagger, but you'll have the true bounty. Pay the vig and get on the list. The public reward is fifty gold so there will be a lot of competition. You deliver the orb to me, and Brar will pay you two hundred gold."

Saria whistled. Fifty gold was one of the highest bounties she'd ever heard, much less two hundred. Even after paying the vig, or the fee for taking the bounty, they'd be set up well. Most bounties paid under twenty gold. Regina wasn't kidding about the interest.

"If you want us to take this ashen orb bounty, why isn't it an exclusive bounty?" Saria asked. "Why the subterfuge?"

"All large bounties go through the system." Regina

shrugged. "I have to enforce the rules so everyone has faith that the system is fair. And it is, or as fair as we can make it. This cuts down on friction between the troops."

"Not for all troops," Saria grumbled, thinking of Skull Posse. But she understood Regina's point. They couldn't have the troops constantly fighting each other when they had a much more important battle against the monsters.

"What do you think?" Regina asked.

There would be representatives from around thirty troops at the faire, and they would all want a shot at it. If they knew the real reward was two hundred gold and involved an enchanted object that would fetch a lot more than two hundred gold on the open market, there would be open warfare over it, so she supposed she understood. "It still seems dishonest. If the other troops find out the truth…"

Regina regarded her evenly. "Is this your way of refusing?"

She wasn't going to refuse, and Regina knew that. "I'm not happy accepting anything from Brar, but we'll do it as a favor to you. I'll need to bring on a replacement for Olive, but the Blades can handle it."

"I know they can," Regina said with a grin.

"Toss me your amulet," Selwyn said. Saria pulled the silver chain that held the sodalite crystal bounty pendant that every troop was issued, the one she now knew Selwyn could track. The mage mumbled a few words and the stone glowed softly. He pulled a scroll out and tossed both to Saria.

Saria held the amulet in her palm, but nothing happened. Normally, any bounties would float above the pendant with what or who was the bounty. "What did you do?"

"Say Brar," Selwyn said.

She did and an image of an orb floated above her palm. She swiped over the stone and a map replaced the first image. An X was marked on the coast.

"According to Brar, you'll find the orb at that locale. The scroll is a map to show your troop. She thinks it is an abandoned temple, but isn't sure," Regina said.

"Isn't sure?"

"She got the information from an oracle, so the details are spotty."

Oracles were notorious for offering half-truths and ambiguous facts, but they usually turned out true, just not how you expected it. She waved her hand over it and the orb reappeared. Placing her hand on the stone stopped the spell. "And this orb is worth two hundred gold?"

"To Brar it is." Regina leaned back in her chair, watching Saria for a long moment. "There's another stipulation."

"I don't like the sound of that."

"You need to tell your troop you're looking for the dagger until you reach the temple. Just in case."

Saria's face heated with annoyance. "Just in case what? Are you saying my people would betray me or the bounty system and steal the orb for themselves?"

"I'm saying you will have two new troop members and Ayre has a certain…reputation." Regina lowered her chin. "It's two hundred gold, Saria. Your troop will forgive you."

Saria considered agreeing but telling her troop the truth anyway. But Regina was right. Jileli seemed trustworthy so far but was new to the group, Ayre wasn't always scrupulously honest, and she had no idea who they'd be adding in Olive's place. "Fine."

Regina sighed and rubbed a hand across her forehead, pausing for another long moment. After resolving whatever internal debate she'd been having, she said, "I also need to request a favor, as a friend. It has nothing to do with the bounties."

"Sure," Saria responded. She drank her whiskey to cover the grimace on her face. Saria hated doing favors, but she wasn't about to turn down the Mistress of Bounties in her own office. She'd protected and trained a wayward girl from an urchin to a Duke's guard to the leader of the Blades. She couldn't turn down any request and they both knew it.

"Chaos Clan ventured into the Ganlam Woods on a bounty to eliminate a necromancer named Lady Calrur. Nasty bitch who wants to take on the Nightmare Queen. They went missing while they were searching for her. Can you keep an eye open for any traces of them? Talos was in the troop when they disappeared."

"I'm sorry." Talos, Regina's only son, was the mage in Chaos Clan. She must be worried sick. Even though Saria had never known her own parents, she understood how gut wrenching losing a child had to be. "I'll keep my eyes and ears open. If I find Talos, I'll bring him home."

At the end of the day, Regina was a mother scared for the safety of her son. "He's probably dead, but I need to know for sure. Your path will take you through the woods, so if you could look."

Saria stood, set her glass on the desk, and nodded to both Regina and Selwyn. "I have things to attend to. I'll see you tomorrow for the faire."

Regina's head lowered, but Saria saw the tears in her eyes. This type of favor was not one she minded in the same way— a personal favor that related to family. Saria owed her on so many levels that returning word of Talos was the least she could do.

The truth was, she'd give her life for Regina. Hopefully, it wouldn't come to that.

The market was packed with people making it hard to navigate the faire as Saria walked toward the recruitment arena. Barefoot children ran in between shoppers, travelers, and troopers with a wild abandon that only the young could pull off. She nodded to the men and women she'd come to know over the past few years since she'd joined the fight against the monsters. While some folk criticized the troops for taking gold to protect them, what else were they supposed to do for food, equipment, and healing potions? They had no idea the toll the troopers paid out in the wilds. The Eylnian Empire had collapsed under the onslaught of monsters, and, for every creature they killed, more took their place. The armies of Southern Holm had been decimated and had never recovered. The troops were the only thing keeping the people from being overrun. Wiser minds than her own liked to theorize how long they would be able to hold out, but all Saria knew was that her last breath would be involved.

Vendors hawked their wares from rolling carts. The main floors of all the buildings boasted sturdy, metal banded doors and no windows. Moonbourne had been breached many times over the years since the fall of the empire, so each building acted as part of the town's fortifications. Large balconies with thick iron cages ran along the second stories of most buildings. The roofs were dotted with archer perches and ranged weapons to help drive off any attackers. While Whitecrest, Ironhold, or any of the larger cities scattered around Southern Holm boasted massive walls with enough troops and defensive weapons to deter monsters, towns like this one did the best they could.

"Saria," a voice called behind her.

She turned to find Trollslayer striding down the street toward her, head and shoulders above the crowd. Hard to miss. She smiled as the big man reached her. "Changed your mind about joining up?"

His laugh was so deep it could start an avalanche. "No, but I saw you and thought you might like some company while you're checking out the new meat."

"Always," Saria said and resumed her walk with the giant beside her. "What's new in town?"

He shrugged. "Same old stuff. Had to break up a brawl between the Ice Tigers and Soulless yesterday. Seems they disagreed over who had completed their last bounty. Turns out Soulless had the rightful claim, but you know how Stog is."

The ogre in question was as mean as a snake and twice as ugly. "He thinks he can bully his way into the upper tiers, but his troopers end up quitting or throwing their lives away."

Trollslayer nodded. "It takes more than brawn to lead a troop."

Saria knew the truth of that. After the old Duke had died, Saria decided to help the people of Southern Holm and not just enhance the position of the duke. It was the one way she could fight back against the monsters. She'd signed on with the Sisters Slay, but Winn, the half-elven warrior who led the group, took too many chances for Saria's liking. After Saria had started her own troop, the Sisters had been killed off trying to capture a rogue naga. "You have to care more for your people than the gold or you won't stay alive long enough to get the gold. Most of them don't understand."

"New blood is cheap," Trollslayer said, disdain thick in his voice. "A good leader keeps their people alive."

"In theory." Her troop did well in that area, Hilo being the most recent exception, though his had been self-inflicted.

They reached the tents that ringed the arena. At one point in history, gladiatorial fights had been all the rage, but now the arena was used for combat practice and try-outs. The

47

city's fighters were too precious to die for entertainment. Prospective troop members showed off their skills in mock battles, and grievances were settled with a minimum of bloodshed. Occasionally, there were grudge matches that resulted in death, but with everything outside the walls trying to kill you, most lost their taste for blood in the arena.

They found a front row bench which groaned under Trollslayer's massive size. He glanced at Saria before sitting on the ground. She stifled a chuckle, not wanting to offend her friend, and turned her attention to the participants in the ring. A human warrior with a long red beard swung his wooden sword at a slim elven woman who danced out of the way easily. She spun her training knives and attacked. To his credit, he held her at bay, barely. Off to the right, a tall shadow fey woman fired a steady stream of arrows into a swinging bucket. The final shot cut the rope in half. Saria applauded.

The woman, with perfectly white hair braided and pulled back, bowed in her direction before retrieving her arrows.

"She can shoot," Saria said.

Trollslayer grunted. "I don't trust the shadow fey."

She nudged his arm with her knee. "You don't trust anyone."

"I trust you."

Saria almost fell off her seat. She was saved when the shadow fey approached the benches. She wore a black jerkin with a silver bird medallion. A scar ran down the side of her neck. Her violet eyes landed on Saria. The shadow fey appraised her like a shopper at market. Given that she halted in front of Saria, she must have seen something good.

"Good afternoon," Saria said.

The fey nodded to them both. "I'm Lithia. I'm looking for a new troop. Do you have an opening on the Blades?"

"You know who I am?" Saria forced the shock out of her

voice. She'd led the Blades for several years, but they were still considered a lower tier than the major troops and more low key than most.

"I do."

"As a matter of fact, we lost our ranger in the last fight we were in."

The woman quirked an eyebrow. "Dead?"

"She's a dryad, so she's healing."

"I would like to join the Blades if you'll have me."

"Why?" popped out of Saria's mouth before she could stop herself.

"The Nat'kran clan leader told me to seek you out. He said the Blades had a good reputation and I would benefit from being with you. You also have a lower death rate than most."

As being a trooper was an exceptionally dangerous profession, she supposed they did. Hilo's death had been an outlier, and then losing Olive not long after—a run of bad luck. Word had spread that Saria was looking for an archer. Regina had told her to be suspicious of her own troop in regard to the ashen orb, what would she think of adding a shadow fey? "May I ask who your leader is?"

"Certainly. His name is Kerza Blightwalker. He had been a member of the Violet Swarm many years ago. He said you were more accepting than some other troops with regard to..." Lithia smiled. "Folk who might normally be shunned."

Beside Saria, Trollslayer grunted. "Folk have their reasons."

"I know," the archer said. "That is why I sought guidance first, and the clan chief was kind enough to offer it."

Interesting. Not that Saria had met many shadow fey—or blood mages, truth be told—but a shadow fey breaking away from their clan to mingle with the rest of the world was not

49

the norm. "We'll be at the bidding tomorrow. Come meet the troop and, if they agree, we'll take you on."

Lithia nodded. "I will see you tomorrow."

Without a word, the shadow fey archer slid into the crowds and vanished.

What were the odds of such a skilled archer seeking her out right when they needed a replacement for their ranger? The other two warriors weren't bad, but Saria preferred to diversify her team. You never knew when a well-placed arrow would be needed. Perhaps it was coincidence that Lithia was at this faire seeking a position on the very day Saria was looking for talent. Given the rumors of the shadow fey shaman's magic, they might have known she would be there.

Too good to be true rang through Saria's mind, but she pushed it aside. Maybe, for once, they'd caught a break.

Looked like they had a new archer, but something still gnawed at Saria's gut. Being dishonest with her troop seemed the most likely cause. Hopefully it was that and not food poisoning again.

10

Saria was up early, wandering around Moonbourne to clear her head before the faire started. Two questions dogged her. One, how was she going to lie to her troop about the orb? And two, more pressing, would Lithia be a good fit for the Blades? Perric certainly wouldn't mind, but Ayre and Jileli might take exception to the inclusion of a shadow fey. The eldar, what the elves called themselves, and others of the fey didn't always get along so well. Given the insane politics among the fey, Saria stayed well away from it.

"Hot lamb pies," a nearby vendor yelled. "Fresh pies, skewers of beef or chicken. Get 'em while they're hot."

Saria's stomach growled at the smells that wafted toward her. An older dwarf stood on a platform that ran along the backside of the cart. He had a steel gray beard down to his knees and a nasty-looking knife in his hand. He didn't look up from turning the sizzling meat from the grill. "Whatcha be havin, lass?"

Lass, huh? It was almost enough to make a girl laugh. She'd been on her own for as long as she could remember.

Her memories of childhood were faint, but she'd been scared and hungry all the time. "Lamb pie sound delicious."

"Three coppers or two fer five," he said. "My wife makes them from scratch. Best you'll find in Moonbourne."

From the scents, she was sure he was right. "I'll take two."

He stepped to the end of the platform, reached into the hot box, and handed Saria two steaming lamb pies. She set a silver coin on the cart. "Keep the change."

The dwarf grinned from ear to ear. "Thanks, I'll buy my wife some flowers with your generous tip."

Saria bit into the fragrant pie. Spiced lamb flooded her palette along with the crisp bite of citrus and a cooling wave of cheese. She groaned in delight.

"I told ye they were the best," the dwarf said with a wink. "My wife is a genius in the kitchen."

"Please give her my compliments," Saria said after she wiped her mouth on her sleeve. "The duke himself doesn't eat this well."

"Well, you run into the boy duke, send him my way."

She smirked at the vendor. "I will." She turned, resuming her walk to the faire. Carts and shops were arranged along the main thoroughfare. People were selling everything from food and weapons to magical trinkets and elixirs that could cure anything and everything. There was even an industrious woman who was selling dragon tooth wards. A dragon hadn't been seen in Saria's lifetime, so she doubted they were real, but the seller did a brisk business.

After a few more streets, and two pies, she reached the faire house. It was a low flat building attached to the training arena at the far end. Troops were arriving at a good clip. According to the sun she was still early, though not as early as she'd planned, but the pies had been worth the delay.

She waved and returned the calls of some of the other troopers. Many she knew by name, but most she identified by the troop they ran with. Soulless, Crimson Dragons, the Unwanted, and many more entered the faire and found seats.

Guards stopped her at the door to check for weapons, which she had left in her room. Technically, the guards would hold your weapons and return them after the faire concluded, but she didn't trust anyone enough to allow that. They didn't find the stiletto in her boot, which was as it should be, and admitted her into the room.

The faire house was easily one hundred feet long and thirty feet wide. Tables were arranged so that troops could sit together and talk. The spaces between allowed the servers to circulate, dropping off food and drink to the raucous troops. Magical torches provided enough light to see by, since the massive fireplaces at either end of the room stood cold.

Perric, Ayre, and Jileli sat at a table on the far side of the room. Ayre was relaying a story that involved a lot of hand gestures and received laughs from the troopers who sat nearby. The scowl on Perric's face told her who the story was about. Jileli sat against the wall, pretending to listen, but her eyes scanned the room. The blood mage nodded when she saw Saria.

"Then his pants fell to his knees, and let's just say the fine ladies and gents of The Velvet Pearl got an eyeful," Ayre said with a flourish.

Perric's face was red as the setting sun, but he kept his mouth shut. Saria had repeatedly told the paladin to ignore Ayre when he was like this, and it seemed he'd finally heeded her advice. Any attempts to divert the thief drove him deeper into his buffoonery.

"Enough," Saria said to Ayre as she took her seat. Poor Perric could only take so much embarrassment, and from the depth of the scarlet on his cheeks, he was nearing his limit. "We have a new recruit coming in today. She's a good shot with a bow. I doubt she has Olive's talents, but we need a fifth if we are taking on bounties."

"Of course, Saria," Jileli said with a faint smile on her face.

"I will warn you, she is a shadow fey." Saria waited for the explosion. None came.

Jileli's quiet acceptance didn't surprise her, since a half succubus could hardly protest a shadow fey, but she was relieved Ayre didn't object. The thief considered for a moment. "We are away from the eldar, so as long as she can pull her weight, I'm fine with it."

Perric grunted. "I've known my fair share of shadow—"

"You mean whores, correct?" Ayre asked, playing up the innocent face. "You know they are only nice to you for your gold, right?"

Perric stiffened, but Jileli stopped the brawl. "Ayre, enough. A funny story is one thing, but insulting the man is a far different matter."

Perric shot the thief a withering look before continuing. "Before the Blades, I traveled with two shadow fey sorcerers, and they were reliable. They always said they weren't vicious enough to live with their clans. Strange taste in food, but they were honorable."

"What would you know about honor?" a voice came from behind Saria.

She turned to find Gnedain from the Skull Posse standing there. "Go find a seat, the faire is about to begin."

"You stole from us, and I'd have my gold back in coin or blood, your choice," the half-orc growled.

"Now see here," Ayre said, starting to rise. Perric pulled the elf back into his seat.

Saria stood, towering over the smaller warrior. He was forced to step back to look her in the eye before his next accusation. "I know it was the leaf muncher. I want our purses back."

"None of my troop took anything belonging to the Skulls," she lied. Normally, she would have made Ayre return the coins, assuming there were any left, but Gnedain's arrogance was too much for her to deal with. "Luckily since the faire is beginning, you'll have a chance to recoup your missing gold by finishing bounties instead of pestering my troop."

The warriors gripped the empty scabbard hanging from his belt. If he had any weapons hidden on him like she did, that would complicate matters. He didn't get a chance to speak as a hand settled over his.

"Saria, is there an issue here?" Lithia asked.

Gnedain's face twisted in pain as Lithia's grip tightened on the half-orc's wrist.

"This is none of your concern," Gnedain said between clenched teeth.

Saria smiled at the leader of the Skulls. "You haven't met our new archer, Lithia. I think that makes it her concern."

"Only a troop as lowly as yours would take on a fey outcast. They say she ran from a fight when she was with Blood Pact."

"She a Blade now," Saria said firmly. She tapped the skull pin on his chest. "Take a seat. The Mistress of Bounties is here."

Lithia released the half-orc's wrist and sat between Saria and Jileli. Gnedain stormed off with the rest of the Skulls in tow. Gnedain was a hothead who didn't lose gracefully. Unfortunately, Ayre's stunt with stealing their purses would inflame his resentment.

The Mistress made her way through the crowds. Selwyn carried a wooden box to the front of the room where he sat it on the table where the bidding would take place. Any troop could buy a bounty, but understanding what your team could handle was more important than the gold you'd make.

Regina, who knew all the troops from the highest tier down to the newest scrubs, reached the front and threw her arms wide. "Greeting, friends!"

The crowd roared back.

"We have a number of bounties, both big and small, today. Without further delay, let the faire begin!"

Shouts went up along with splashes of ale from hastily raised mugs. The room quieted as Selwyn described the first bounties of the day. "First up, we've got a rampaging axe breaker south of Auano. The town is paying five gold for eliminating the beast. The vig is three silvers."

A young gnome stood on his chair. He wore bulbous goggles on his forehead and carried a large wrench in his belt. "The Broken Gears will accept the bounty."

The room erupted in a mixture of cheers and catcalls. The gnome jumped down, paid Selwyn the silvers, and handed over his bounty amulet to Selwyn. The mage spoke a few words and the crystal glowed. The amulet was returned, and the gnome activated it. The image of the axe breaker and then a map appeared. Once the gnome's troop killed the monster, they would take proof to the requester and collect their bounty. Two other troops paid the vig, had their amulets enchanted, and the bidding went on.

Saria listened to each bounty and conferred with the team. This early in the day, the bounties weren't worth the time it would take the Blades to fulfill them. Newer or smaller troops jumped at the chance to eliminate an owl bear or a couple feral centaurs. There wasn't always much competition for those smaller bounties since there wasn't much gold involved, so the newer troops didn't have to worry that another more experienced troop would beat them to the take. Many troops also bid on multiple bounties, though doing so meant you risked other troops getting there first.

After a few hours and a lot of ale, the Mistress reached

the higher coin bounties. Primal Watch took an exclusive bounty to remove a minotaur from near the dwarven city of Ironhold, meaning the town only wanted one troop on the job and Primal Watch outbid everyone else.

Since Chaos Clan's disappearance, Primal, at diamond level, was the highest ranked on the bounty board. The Blades were still in silver, but the Skulls had moved to gold, much to Saria's irritation. Outside of bragging rights, rankings affected what type of talent you attracted and whether you could afford to outbid others on exclusives.

"The next bounty is to retrieve a stolen dagger. It is a family heirloom, and the owner wants it back and is willing to pay fifty gold for its return. The owner tracked it to Tolle. The vig is a single gold coin."

"I offer five gold for exclusive rights," Gnedain shouted from the other side of the room. He shot Saria a smug look. "The Skull Posse will deliver the dagger."

Oh, here we go.

11

Saria stood as did a number of the other troops in the silver and gold ranks. "The Blades will pay the vig for the job."

"The Skulls have laid claim to the exclusive rights," Gnedain said, trying to talk over the other troops, who were now shouting their acceptance of the bounty. The fact that the Skulls weren't liked probably drove as many bids as the reward.

"Quiet!" Selwyn bellowed over all the bickering troops. "The Mistress will address the issue. Sit down or be thrown out!"

Saria glanced back to where Trollslayer and his guards stood. The giant had a stout club the size of a roof support beam in his hand. He noticed her looking and winked. Saria stifled a laugh and sat.

"Thank you, Selwyn. While not unheard of to request an exclusive on a bounty, I will not be granting—"

Gnedain leapt to his feet. "This is an outrage."

Regina arched an eyebrow at the outburst.

Triz, the lizard-man mage, whispered in his leader's ear

before pulling him back into his seat. Trollslayer lumbered over to the Skull Posse table.

"If he shouts out again, please remove him from the faire and the Skull Posse will be dropped to copper ranking," the Mistress said to Trollslayer, glaring at Gnedain. "Do you understand?"

"Yes, Mistress. The Skulls will follow your rules." Gnedain scowled around the room as if tempting anyone to mock him. No one did, but that was out of respect, or fear, of the Mistress.

"Excellent," she said before resuming what she was saying. "The information the benefactor has acquired tells us that a group of thieves stole the dagger and is planning on taking it off continent. The benefactor also did not request an exclusive bounty. Given these facts, the Keeper of Records and I decided that more troops are better to ensure it doesn't leave on a ship. I made arrangements with the Tolle harbor master to delay departing ships for three days. Your bounty will have all the details including an image of the dagger."

"Any questions for the Mistress?" Selwyn asked the crowd. No one answered.

Saria kept her face as blank as possible so as not to reveal anything more than anyone else might be feeling. Knowing their team had a secret exclusive on the true bounty while the other troops would be spinning their daggers in Tolle felt wasteful. Those troops could be defending villages and stopping hordes instead, but Regina was right about one thing. Considering what an asshole Gnedain had already been about the fake dagger, a bounty for an actual enchanted artifact might cause a riot.

"The vig is a gold piece. The leaders may approach," Regina said.

Ayre flipped a gold coin to Saria to pay for the vig. The thief had turned out to be somewhat of a financial genius. He took care of all the expenses for the troop. How much of their funds were from after-hours thievery, Saria wasn't sure, but there were some things better left unknown.

And even with Ayre's less than law-abiding love for gold, she hated that Regina didn't want her to trust him and the others with the truth.

She handed the coin to Selwyn, who took her amulet and enchanted it with the bounty, and then passed it to her. A hand grabbed Saria's wrist and pulled. Saria jerked her arm free and turned on Gnedain. The half-orc might be shorter than Saria, but he was built like a minotaur.

"I want to see that bounty. There is something going on and I don't like it," Gnedain said, a snarl twisting his tusked mouth into a hideous grimace.

"Are you doubting the honesty of bounty system?" the mistress asked.

Selwyn rolled his eyes. "Saria, give him the amulet. Let him and everyone else see that we do not play favorites when we grant bounties."

She tossed the amulet to Gnedain. He studied it for a second before setting it flat on his palm. "Open."

An image of the dagger in question hovered over the amulet. The Skull Posse leader scrolled through the contents of the enchanted piece. A map, the bounty writ, and a crudely drawn sketch of some people who were presumably the thieves floated into being at each command. "It looks normal."

Saria snatched it back. "I don't know what your problem is, but go find someone who fucking cares," Saria said, trying to force down the urge to stab this asshole. Unfortunately, doing so would reveal that she was breaking the rules with her boot dagger. She turned to return to her table.

"This isn't over, bitch." Gnedain paid the vig and Selwyn

enchanted the Skull's amulet. He checked it to make sure it matched what Saria had.

"That is one fucked up orc," Lithia said. "We'll need to keep an eye on him."

"Spoken like a true Shadow Blade," Perric said with a chuckle. "I would have paid good coin to see the Mistress drop them to copper status."

"We need to leave as soon as the faire concludes," Saria said in a low voice. Worry flooded her mind as ideas that the true bounty had somehow gotten to the Skull Posse. The half-orc was a flaming asshole, but he was playing it loose with the Mistress and that was concerning. "Gnedain will be looking to cause trouble if we stay in town. Better to be away from it."

"Looks like they have a similar idea," Jileli said.

The Skull Posse followed Gnedain out of the building. While not against the rules of the faire to leave before it was over, it was unusual enough to garner comments from the other troops.

"What was all that about?" Ayre asked. The thief spun a spoon in his fingers like he would his dagger if he had it with him. "Must be trying to get a head start on the bounty."

"Gnedain is a sore loser." Perric started to say more, but the Mistress called the next bounty.

An hour later, the Faire ended. Each bounty was now listed on the troop standing board, where it irked her to see the Skulls hadn't been put in cooper. If they completed this bounty, it would move them into the same rank as the Skulls. That would chap Gnedain's ass, for sure.

The Blades returned to the inn. Saria pointed at a table in the corner. Ayre went off to get mugs of ale while the team settled in. After the thief slid drinks to each of the team, he struck up a conversation with their newest member. "So,

Lithia, tell us why you want to join the Blades, other than my striking good looks?"

She took a swallow from her mug. "Saria said you need an archer and I happen to be one. I've heard you run a good troop and are up and coming."

That story tracked with what she'd told Saria yesterday. Nothing suspicious so far.

"You don't have a problem with two eldar?" Jileli said.

"Two? I get that pretty boy is a full blood, but I've never seen an eldar with horns, to be blunt. You must be a mix." She took another drink. "I'm an outcast from the shadow fey, so unless you have an issue with me, I'd be happy to join."

Perric wiped his mouth on his sleeve. "He's not that pretty, but as long as you pull your weight in a fight, you are good with me."

"I'm not that pretty?" Ayre asked, mock indignation thick in his voice. "I'm fucking beautiful. Diamonds lose their luster when I'm around."

"Ayre," Saria said, rubbing her head. "Yea or nay?"

"Other than being wounded to the quick, I'm good," the thief said, flashing a brilliant smile at Lithia.

"Jileli?" Saria asked. The blood mage was also new, so she wasn't sure how this would play out.

"Place your hand in mine, please," Jileli said. She held her hand out toward Lithia. "Do I have your consent to perform a harmless spell?"

"It's not a loyalty test, is it?" Lithia joked.

"Not exactly. But it is a test of sorts."

"Sure, I'm good at tests."

The archer did as asked. Her eyes widened when blood oozed from the back of her hand. The droplets danced in a wild pattern, rising and falling like motes in a storm. The power sang in Saria's ears like a siren's call. How strange that she responded to Jileli's magic when she never did to anyone else's. After a few seconds, the blood seeped back into the archer's hand.

Lithia snatched her hand and examined it closely. Not a scratch showed what had happened. "What did you do to me?"

"That was an example of my magic," Jileli answered. "Now you know what you are dealing with. While I can do other spells, I am primarily a blood mage. I use demonic powers to fight my enemies and heal my friends. Do you trust me enough to join?"

Still rubbing at her hand, Lithia nodded. "Aye, if you'll have me, I'd be honored."

Saria drained her mug and set it on the table. "Done. Welcome to the troop, Lithia."

The others cheered their newest member.

"Two hours and we head out of town," Saria said. "We need to discuss our plans, but not here."

"Why?" Perric frowned, no doubt missing a second night at The Velvet Pearl.

"Let's just say things seem a bit odd with this bounty. I don't want anything to go wrong."

Saria hated keeping information from the troop, but she at least had to tell everyone they weren't going to Tolle. If the true bounty leaked, any hint of it, it could jeopardize both the Mistress and the Blades. The Skulls already seemed primed for a fight, and the walls in Moonbourne sometimes had ears.

It was time to go.

12

The troop gathered at the front of the inn before setting out. When everyone was assembled, Saria led the troop out the far entrance of the town and across the stone bridge that ran over the Serpent River, headed for Tolle like everyone else. They made good progress over the next couple of hours. Lithia took the lead and Saria brought up the rear.

Once into the forest, they diverted off the broken road and found a place to camp for the night. Jileli placed wards around the clearing while the rest set up a small fire and prepared a dinner of beef and potatoes. Lithia took over cooking, and within a half an hour, they were eating around the fire.

"Where did you learn to cook like this?" Perric asked after he devoured his food. "That might be the best camp grub I've ever had."

"After the nexus portals were opened and the monsters destroyed our lands, we had to move a lot, so it was important to have good food. Our art, culture, and livelihoods were gone, and my people were forced to flee, but we retained our love of cooking. Now that my people have established a new home, they are reestablishing our culture."

"I'd heard the shadow fey had fled to the west," Jileli said while scraping her plate into the fire. "All of the races of Southern Holm were forced to change after the Eylnian Empire collapsed."

"The eldar held their lands, but the losses were catastrophic. I lost my father and siblings in the war," Ayre said softly. The thief rarely shared anything personal. It astounded Saria that he opened up about it.

"I'm sorry, Ayre," Saria said.

He cleared his throat as if shocked by his own admission. "Well, enough of that. What was going on with Gnedain at the bidding? Why did he care about your amulet so much?"

"He seemed to think that the bounty was being handled differently from the others," Jileli said. "I may be new, but everyone knows the bounties must be offered to all unless the benefactor themselves asks for an exclusive."

"Maybe he just wanted to fondle your goods," Ayre said with a wicked grin.

Saria shuddered. "That is one image I don't need in my head. Please keep your disgusting ideas to yourself."

Ayre laughed.

"Seriously," Perric said. "I get that Ayre relieved them of their purses, but to stop the transfer of a bounty is unheard of. What game is he playing at?"

"I don't know." Regina had asked Saria to wait until they reached the temple to tell her team the whole truth, but they would still need to go to the temple, which was a different direction than the troops after the fake dagger. She pulled out the map Selwyn had given her and rolled it out on the ground.

"What's this?" Ayre asked.

"Where we are actually going," Saria said. "I'm going to

ask you to trust me and know I've always got the Blades' best interest in mind."

"That's not Tolle," Perric remarked.

"By all the gods above and below, he's right!"

"Enough, Ayre." Saria pointed to the X on the map, the possible temple. "Our destination is here."

"Why did the Mistress tell everyone to go to Tolle then?" Lithia asked.

"I can't answer that yet."

"And we are just supposed to follow along?" Lithia asked.

"Or head back to Moonbourne." Saria looked at each of them in turn. "I have told you as much as I can. It is still a bounty. I can't give you the details."

"Why?" Perric asked.

Damn Regina for putting her in this position. It felt as wrong as she feared it would, but at the same time, she didn't know Jileli well and didn't know Lithia at all. "Ayre and Perric already know this, but I'll share this with our new members so they'll understand. Regina isn't just the Mistress of the Bounties to me. We have a long-standing relationship from when we were both with Duke Nalan, and she asked me to wait. She also asked me to follow up any leads on her son Talos, who's gone missing. He's in Chaos Clan. What say you?"

Perric scratched at his beard. "I don't like it, but I'm in."

Jileli and Lithia agreed as well. Saria's gaze turned to Ayre.

"Fifty gold is still a lot of coin. I'm in."

Saria let out a sigh of relief. "Thank you. I will explain in full, but are there any other questions?"

"Are you not telling us because I'm shadow fey?" Lithia asked. Her eyes were locked on the ground as she spoke.

"Not one bit." Saria hated that Lithia felt that way, but it couldn't be avoided.

"Why do you ask?" Ayre studied Lithia for a long time, but Saria couldn't tell why.

"Like what you see?" Lithia asked.

Ayre shrugged. "That will have to wait until I see you use that bow of yours. But that doesn't answer my question, now does it?"

She laughed. "My people are generally regarded as evil and untrustworthy. If Saria didn't trust me at all, I'd head back to Moonbourne and find a different troop."

"I trust you all," Saria said. "I hate keeping anything from the troop, but out of respect, I'm doing as I was asked."

Perric took the map from Saria. They plotted their path along the river until they reached the Nathal Bridge to cross to the northern shore. From there a dotted trail led to whatever was at the X on the bounty map. There wasn't anything marked on the crudely drawn parchment in that area, but that was where they were headed. It was on the ocean shore but in a remote part of Southern Holm.

"We are three or four days from there. Perric has first watch, I'll take second, then Jileli, Ayre, and Lithia," Saria said, placing the map back into her rucksack. "Any questions?"

They all shook their heads. Each one laid out their camp roll and got ready for bed. Perric pulled the winged sword from the sheath and set to polishing it while he took his turn on watch.

Saria fell asleep to the soft whisper of the cleaning cloth.

Around midnight, Perric woke Saria, stripped off his armor, and rolled into his blankets. The sword was never far from his hand. Saria stepped away from the burning coals of their earlier campfire. If anything happened, she didn't want the light to mess up her sight.

She patrolled the edge of the clearing, staying clear of the wards while listening to the sounds of the night. Insects and night birds sang their songs, woodland creatures scurried about, and the whispering wind played in the trees. Everything was as it should be.

Saria couldn't get the unusualness of this bounty out of her head. It was unlike Regina to handpick a troop for a job, even given their close relationship. There had never been any favors or special treatment for her or the troops she was in. Why was she the one Brar wanted or had Regina made that choice? What had stood out to make either think only Saria could be trusted to retrieve an enchanted object? She had barely interacted with Brar in the past and hadn't wanted to, not with the sorceress's reputation.

Ironically, Saria knew she could be trusted. She had no use for enchanted objects herself, and the two hundred gold Brar had offered was sufficient. But it still bothered her. All of it.

The world was full of mysteries, and this was another of them. Even when they retrieved the pretend dagger, the Blades would move up the board given the amount of coin and the difficulty of the bounty.

With advanced levels came….

Crack! came from the woods on the far side of the clearing from her.

Saria froze. She crouched behind a deadfall and watched the clearing. Nothing happened. She waited.

Perric rolled over in his sleep, mumbling something incoherent, while the rest slumbered on. Her mind said it wasn't anything but a broken branch falling, but her intuition after years of adventuring told her something was wrong.

When no other noises came, she scanned the tree line

around the clearing and caught a flicker of motion. Someone, or something, was in the woods thirty feet across from her. By her feet, she found a small pebble. Careful not to be seen, she tossed the stone through the night. It landed next to Ayre's head. The elf flinched but didn't call out. Saria skulked along the tree line so she could see Ayre's face and pointed to where the threat was coming from.

Another flicker of motion. Whatever was out there was close to the camp.

Ayre coughed, then rolled on his side. Jileli's head bobbed slightly. The wards must have woken her. Perric's hand closed over the hilt of his sword. Lithia's bow was already next to the archer, but her hand now rested next to her quiver.

Saria didn't take her gaze off the place where the motion had come from, willing something to happen. A moment later, Gnedain and the rest of the Skulls charged into the clearing.

"Now, we'll see who is the stronger troop," Gnedain said as his team rushed the sleeping Blades.

He'd find out, all right, after Saria removed his head.

13

The clearing exploded into action. Perric leapt to his feet, meeting the charging Skulls. A massive clang rang out as he parried an axe swing from the dwarven attacker he faced.

Saria pulled her long sword and dirk from their sheaths and rushed to the aid of her companions. The twang of Lithia's bowstring sang and a darkened form of one of the Skull Posse dropped to the ground.

"I'll kill you!" Gnedain shouted as he closed the distance between them. He swung his broadsword at Saria but she slid under the stroke and sliced open the leather armor across his ribs with her dirk. She spun and caught his second strike on her sword. The blow numbed her hand for a moment, but she held onto her weapon through sheer force of will.

A streak of red illuminated the clearing, courtesy of Jileli. Gnedain's face was twisted in rage under his half helm. His tusks gleamed with spit that dripped down his chin. The dwarf still engaged Perric to her right, and Ayre wove an intricate dance with the Skulls elven assassin. Knives darted in and out, mostly hitting air. A red bolt from Jileli slammed into the lizard-man's shield spell.

Gnedain's head swung to see what the spell had hit.

Saria took Gnedain's moment of distraction to kick him in the knee. The warrior stumbled, and she stabbed at his chest. No matter how much of a hothead Gnedain was, he could hold his own in a fight. The half-orc pivoted, taking a glancing blow on the shoulder. He threw himself away from Saria and rolled across the ground.

The oldest trick in the book. Saria waited for her opponent to gain his feet. In the arena, Gnedain used that feint to chop the legs out from under any unsuspecting opponent who ran in to finish the fight. With a practice sword, he'd broken a couple legs. The broadsword would completely remove them.

Gnedain grunted in frustration. The arena had dulled his skills in a real fight with a skilled opponent. He raised his sword and charged again. Another vivid red bolt from Jileli slammed into his chest, driving him back.

"Why the fuck are you attacking us?" Saria asked. "Troops don't fight other troops. We lose enough to the monsters."

"You've cheated the system. I was willing to pay for exclusive rights," Gnedain said, swinging his sword back and forth.

Saria paced to the side warily, watching the half-orc's body instead of his face. "That isn't your decision to make. We all play by the same rules."

The half-orc stiffened. "You are her prized pet. She denied us because you get special treatment!"

"Bullshit. You know the rules, but you only apply them when it suits you," Saria said. "Call off your troop before it's too late."

Gnedain looked around. One of his troopers was already dead. The dwarf was barely holding off Perric. Ayre was toying with the Skull's assassin. "I'll die before I yield to you."

"So be it."

They charged each other. Saria caught the heavier broadsword between her longsword and dirk. She kicked Gnedain's leg, and he stumbled. Before he could recover, she spun, taking him full on the left shoulder with her sword. Blood sprayed as the blade bit between his pauldron and rerebrace. Leather armor was tough, but if you knew how it worked, there were gaps.

The half-orc screamed, more out of rage than pain. He swung again, and Saria deflected the heavier sword with her two blades. A volley of arrows peppered the warrior as he stumbled back.

Not waiting for Gnedain to recover, Saria swung hard at his exposed neck. He flopped to the ground and rolled away. Unlike the first, this was more like a fish landing on dry land.

"Stop!" a sibilant voice called from behind Saria. She turned to see Triz with his knife at Lithia's throat. The shadow fey looked more bored than worried. "Lay down your weapons or I kill her."

Ayre laughed. "She recently joined the Blades. Do you think we care if you kill her? Especially since we can make your final moments oh so painful."

Triz's tongue flickered out in a sign of panic. "Gnedain was wrong to attack the Blades, but—"

"But nothing," Jileli said. The blood mage cast the spell she's been preparing. Triz's eyes went wide as the weaves of red and black hit him. He screamed once as his life force flowed into the succubus. She purred as the lizard-man dropped to the ground, a mere husk of a man.

Lithia brushed off her shoulder where Triz had held her. "Thanks for the assist."

Jileli's eyes glowed a strong purple color. "My pleasure."

Saria swallowed hard. Gnedain was nowhere to be found. The rest of the Skulls were dead around the clearing. Bar brawls and the occasional duel were to be expected, but a full out assault was unheard of. She'd have to tell the Mistress when they returned what happened. Saria amended it in her head. *If we return.*

"So much for a good night's sleep," Ayre chuckled. "Stoke the fire so we can see."

"What would have made another troop attack us like this" Perric said, not looking at the corpses strewn around the clearing. The bodies were scattered like a child's broken toys. "Petty grievances are not worth the loss of life. This is not righteous behavior."

"I don't think the Skulls are big on righteousness." Saria wiped down her hands and wondered for the fiftieth time if she should tell the team the truth about their bounty. Was that the true reason the Skulls had come after them? Or was Gnedain really that vindictive? She would have thought he'd have been more interested in getting a head start to Tolle instead of tracking them when they veered off course.

"I can see that traveling with the Blades is going to be exciting. What do we do with the bodies?" Lithia asked.

"We leave the bodies for Gnedain," Saria said. "That is, if he has the honor to come back for his dead."

"Any reason we can't see if there is anything of value?" Ayre's gaze flickered to the body of the assassin he'd killed in the fight.

"You disgust me." Perric's face flushed red. "Those were fellow troopers—"

"Who tried to kill us all," Jileli said softly. "They would have taken everything if they had won."

Perric snorted. "Well, it hardly surprises me that the demon—"

"She's right," Lithia said from the upturned log she used as a stool. Her bow was across her knees as she worked on it. "The Skulls didn't have to attack us. There was no reason, and they knew the consequence of their actions. Gnedain could have crawled off somewhere to die alone, so why leave useful bits to rot out here?"

Perric stammered. He searched for the words, but Saria put an end to it.

"Enough. Ayre, check for anything of value, but it is a group loot. Make sure you grab those damned skull emblems so we can prove they attacked. We'll divide up what we find. Perric, can you check the perimeter for signs of Gnedain? If he comes back, I want warning."

"The first reasonable thing that's been said." Perric drew his winged sword and stomped away from the rest. When he entered the forest, Saria turned to Jileli.

"If you need to 'harvest' anything for your spells, Jileli, now is the time," Saria said. "I don't want Perric to see. No need riling him up any more than he is."

"Understood." Jileli pulled a small ornate knife and a leather wallet from her pack and went to the fallen lizard-man. She made quick work of draining blood and removing pieces from the corpse.

Lithia turned to Saria. "How is it you are working with a blood mage? Most people find them distasteful at best, and in some places, they're killed on sight."

Saria thought it was interesting that Lithia asked that considering that most people felt the same about shadow fey. She glanced at where Jileli perched over the dwarf Perric had bested. Her horns glowed a subtle purple. She wielded her knife like a master surgeon. "She can't help what she is any more than any of us. She's honest, trustworthy, and tough in a scrap. Her magic saved our ranger's life and our butts."

"Will you look at this?" Ayre said from where he rummaged through the assassin's kit. He held up an open pine box. "If the labels are correct, there are poisons I've only heard rumors of are in here."

Saria rolled her eyes. "Kid in a candy store."

Lithia laughed. "Can you blame him? The assassin guilds are tightlipped about their wares."

Jileli returned to the fire. She held out a bag to Saria. "All set. It is easier to have, err, supplies on hand than rely on my own blood so much. I also found these."

Saria hefted the bag. The contents shifted and clanked together. "What are they?"

"Unlimited light stones," Jileli said with a smile. "The Skulls must have spent a fortune on them."

"Serves them right." Saria untied the drawstring and light flooded out the opening. Oh, wow. These stones were one of the hottest scores in the troops. No one knew how to recreate them, so there were a limited number. How had the Skulls come to own them? The only ones she'd ever seen in person were the ones that belonged to Chaos Clan. Talos liked to use them to make shadow puppets, of all things. One of the benefits of growing up with one of the most powerful mages around.

Her brain instantly tried to make a connection between Regina's fears about Talos and the Skulls having these stones, but there was no way the Skulls could have bested Chaos Clan. There was no telling where the stones had come from, but now they belonged to the Blades.

The sounds of Perric crashing through the forest reached them before the paladin stepped into the clearing. He too held a leather pouch. "Saria, we've got trouble."

"What do you mean?" Saria got up and went to where Perric stood.

He handed her the pouch. "I think that's Gnedain's. You might want to look inside."

Saria pursed her lips and opened the bag. Ayre snatched it from her grasp. "Allow me, our wonderful leader. You never know when traps are left for the unwary."

Perric humphed. "I opened it, and nothing happened."

Ayre smiled at Perric like he was a simple child. The elf sat on the ground and upended the pouch. A few coins, a couple of gems, and a half-carved piece of wood tumbled out. Ayre shook the bag; a puff of gray dust and two nondescript markers joined the rest. "Interesting."

Perric reached down, but Ayre's hand slapped him away. "They are covered in a residue. Jileli, can you see what it is?"

"I already touched it, it's fine," Perric said.

Jileli sat next to Ayre. "They are warded with what looks like death magic. Given that these markers are used by the assassin's guild, they are probably tuned to Gnedain so that he can touch them but will trigger if anyone else does."

"It didn't hurt me," Perric said again.

"You've got gauntlets on." Jileli fished out her leather wallet and unrolled it next to her. Vials of differing shapes and sizes were in individual compartments. "If you'd have touched it with your skin, you'd be dead."

The big man blanched. He bent and rubbed his hands through the dirt, muttering curses under his breath.

"So, these are death markers." It wasn't a question. They were given to assassins to mark their targets, and the Skulls having them made no sense. "I know they had an assassin on the team, but why would a troop be taking jobs from the guild?"

"That remains to be seen." The blood mage pulled out a vial filled with a viscous green liquid. The odor drove everyone away when she pulled the cork.

"That's disgusting," Lithia said, holding her nose. "What is that stuff?"

"Troll blood." Jileli trickled the blood around the contents of the pouch. When she joined the ends, the circle burst with a green light. Jileli chanted in a language Saria didn't know. She opened a second vial and dribbled milky white liquid on the amulets. Smoke erupted from the tokens. When it cleared, Jileli broke the circle and retrieved the items. "They are safe now."

Saria accepted the pieces. On the surface, they looked like bounty amulets, but they weren't. The metal shone with a darkness that the normal ones didn't have. The symbols etched into the metal made Saria want to throw them into the woods and run. "Can you tell me more about these?"

"We call them te'naloth," Lithia said. The archer's eyes held a trace of fear. "They are rumored to be able to track an assassin's target anywhere in the land."

Saria took the first and laid it in her palm. "Open."

A soft light emerged from the black stone in the center. Perric whistled when the face resolved. "That's Karfer, the leader of Chaos Clan. Why would they be hunting the troop's leader?"

"Next," Saria said, looping through the other four members of Chaos Clan. Her stomach tightened with every familiar face. "They are hunting all of them."

"Do you think the Skulls are behind Chaos Clan being missing?" Perric said. I can't see that happening. Gnedain's troop would have gotten destroyed in a head-on battle."

Ayre snorted. "The Skulls would stoop to any level to make coin. They could have poisoned the troop and then finished them off once they were out of it."

Saria's stomach fell the rest of the way to her feet. She'd promised to find word of Talos, but this wasn't the news she'd hoped to deliver. The Skulls having the light stones seemed to prove it.

"What's on the other one?" Ayre asked.

Saria tossed the first amulet to Ayre and set the second in her palm. "Open."

When the shape coalesced, Saria saw her own face looking back at her.

"Well, fuck."

14

A re the rest of us in there?" Ayre asked.

"Next."

Perric's face shimmered into view. Where Saria's picture had been carefully drawn, Perric's was not. The big man huffed. "Who drew that, a five-year-old?"

"I'm thinking a drunk gnome with at least one eye missing," Ayre said, laughing at his own joke.

"Next."

Ayre's image appeared. The artist was far more skilled than whoever had drawn Perric.

"Well, they know true beauty when they see it, though my nose is much more regal than this hack can pull off," Ayre said with a lot of hand waving. He was never at a loss for dramatics.

"Next."

"Oh, that's not good," Jileli said, her hand over her mouth. "Do I look so awful?"

The artist had taken vast liberties, turning the beautiful Jileli into a horned monster. Fangs, which she didn't have, reached her chin. Her eyes were huge and looked evil.

Anyone walking past the blood mage would never have recognized her from this drawing. Could it be that the artist had never actually seen Jileli and was guessing?

"No, you don't," Perric answered. "While I don't agree with your magic, you are no monster. People demonize that which they don't understand."

Ayre stared at the paladin. "Who are you?"

Perric shrugged. His face flushed a bright pink. "We are the Shadow Blades, and we stick together. I might not like the use of blood in magic, but she's fighting to save people."

"Thank you, Perric," Jileli said, though her eyes were still locked on the image.

"Next."

Olive's face was the last to appear. The ranger had her telltale smirk. The artist had taken a lot of time detailing her beauty. Her portrait was the most expertly drawn of all five of them.

"Well, that's good news." Ayre gestured to the image of Olive. "They don't know that Olive isn't with us and Lithia is. This means the marker was created after we hired Jileli but before we attended the troop faire. And it still doesn't answer why anyone would put a death mark on us."

"It has to be something to do with Chaos Clan," Saria said, sorting through the rapid-fire thoughts that poured through her head. She closed her hand and the image of Olive winked out of existence. She'd never heard of a troop being marked for death, let alone two.

"The main connection between us and Clan Chaos is the Mistress," Ayre offered. "Talos is her son, and you knew her before."

"You think someone wants to target the Mistress of Bounties?" Perric said.

"I don't know why they would do it like this." Something was going on behind the scenes but she didn't think it had anything to do with the ashen orb bounty. Chaos Clan had been missing for three months and Regina had only received the request from Brar recently. "Though it doesn't seem like a coincidence that Gnedain had death marks for both troops."

"The biggest questions are who is behind the assassination request and if there are any more assassins looking for us." Lithia had retrieved her arrows and examined each carefully before replacing them in her quiver. "Fuck, I lost two arrows. I'll have to make more if we keep getting attacked."

"The good news is we are headed to a location far from where the rest of the troops were sent. That should give us cover until we can determine who is paying for our deaths," Saria said. "Unless of course the assassins can track us."

"We should move to a new campsite before Gnedain comes back, if he even has enough honor to bury his own dead." Perric had cleaned and sheathed his sword. The big man set off for the trail they'd been following.

"Are you limping?" Jileli asked.

Perric turned. "Twisted my ankle, fighting the dwarf. That axe was tough to defend against."

"I can heal it," Jileli said. Her eyes dropped to the ground.

Perric studied the blood mage for a moment before he answered. "I appreciate it, but it isn't broken, just sore."

"That's twice now. What did you do with Perric?" Ayre asked.

The paladin lifted his eyes to the sky. "You are tiring, Ayre."

Ayre pulled off a perfect court bow. "It is my goal to keep things lively."

"Let's go," Saria said before the two started bickering. Perric took the lead, with Ayre and Jileli behind him. Lithia hung back by Saria.

"Mind if I walk with you?" The archer had her bow in her hand and a worried look on her face.

"Sure. What's on your mind?"

"What happened before you got to Moonbourne? Anything that would make you the target of assassins?"

Saria ran down the bounty they had completed before heading to Moonbourne, the kobold attack, and the run-in with the troll. "I needed to find a replacement for Olive, and you fit the bill. I can't imagine any of that would have run us afoul of the assassin's guild unless that troll we killed was their secret weapon."

"You were busy," Lithia said with a chuckle. "I ran with a couple smaller troops before reaching Moonbourne. We cleaned up the country around Auano. No bounties, just a bit of coin. When the last group disbanded, I thought it was time to try the big leagues."

"Why not one of the stronger troops? The Blades aren't in the upper tiers. Hell, the Skulls are higher than we are."

"Not anymore." Lithia shot Saria a grin. "Gnedain approached me about a spot on his team, but I would have had to fuck the orc to get it. That was...less than appealing."

Saria cringed. Rumors said the half-orc's taste went to the extremes. To each his own, but what she'd heard had turned her stomach. "Well, none of that with the Blades."

"I guess I signed with you at the right time. We get to play hide and seek with assassins while on a secret bounty you can't tell us about," Lithia said. "Unless you want to tell us now?"

"I can't yet." She did understand why her clan leader would have recommended them in normal times. Far too many teams refused to work with shadow fey or half-succubi or a number of other races. Saria let the person's ability talk for them. Well, except for bards. You had to have some stan-

THE ASHEN ORB BOUNTY

dards. "We are glad to have you. Assassins or no assassins. You can use that bow."

"Thanks. What happens when Olive returns?"

Saria considered the question. Most troops stuck to five members. It gave you enough firepower but didn't split the coin you earned too many ways. Most bounties were manageable with five skilled adventures since over time the troops had thinned out the worst of the monsters. When the job was harder, it wasn't unheard of for troops to combine forces. Olive had been with the Blades since the inception and had many skills beyond her bow. It might be worth the extra cost to have both on the team. "We'll burn that bridge when we come to it. Olive could be communing with the tree for decades."

Lithia smiled. "Well then, let's kick some ass."

Shadow fey had a reputation for being difficult to deal with and arrogant to boot. Lithia had said she was an outcast. Maybe it was because she was modest and levelheaded? Who had ever heard of a modest fey of any sort? Look at Ayre. Whatever the reason, her skills with the bow helped the troop stay alive.

Between the bounty and the assassins, that was becoming more challenging by the day.

⁕

After two uneventful days of walking and camping, Perric signaled for a halt. Saria moved past Jileli and Ayre, leaving Lithia to cover the rear. The archer had already nocked an arrow as she watched behind the troop.

The trees had grown more bent the closer they grew to the ocean, mostly pines and bramble. Here, the forest thinned out, and the brush grew heavier without the pine needle carpet. Perric stood near a large tree, waiting. When

Saria walked next to him, he pointed. "My guess is that is our destination."

The path led up a large hill to a massive stone temple. Statues covered in ivy and lichen stood sentinel at the opening of the crumbling cobblestone path. Smaller structures that looked like guard towers sat at the switchback that led to the main building. A broken idol sat atop the partially collapsed structure. Monsters, war, and a century of disuse had degraded the temple to the point of ruin.

"From the looks of the statues, my guess is this was a temple of Insus. The god of the hunt was powerful in the old empire, not so much now," Perric said.

"I didn't know this was out here," Jileli said from behind Saria. "It is immense."

"The disciples of Insus knew how to throw a party," Ayre said. "This one time when I was a strapping young lad, wet behind the ears but eager to—"

"Not now, Ayre." Saria studied the temple with the cracked and broken pillars and the worn steps. Darkness was settling in, going from the day into the night. Fallen temples were never places one wanted to wander into unprepared. In fact, as she studied the intimidating ruins, her stomach sank along with the sun. "Let's camp away from here. I want to see it in full light before we approach it."

And she wanted to consider when it was the right time to tell the troop they were seeking an enchanted orb for Brar Opalback and not an heirloom dagger.

"Makes sense," Ayre said, though the elf pouted at not being allowed to tell his story.

"Once we get settled, you can tell your stories about Insus. There may be knowledge we need to find this thing to complete the bounty and get the hell out of here," Saria said.

"Then what are we waiting for?" Ayre said. His tone reminded Saria of a small child given a treat.

"I saw a good spot back a few minutes," Lithia said. "We should be far enough away."

"Lead the way, my lady," Ayre said with a courtly bow.

Lithia headed into the forest with Jileli and Ayre in tow. A temple this large would have had a village built up around it, but whatever was left would be nearly invisible as the sun set. Perric held on to Saria's shoulder. While Saria could see like a cat in the dark, she'd found other humans lacked that ability.

"You had to encourage him?" Perric said with a chuckle. "You know he'll talk all night."

"I do, but it will distract me from thinking about the temple. Nothing about this situation feels right. From Chaos Clan's disappearance, to the Mistress hand-picking us to take this bounty, to the Skull Posse attack, to the death markers. Forces are at play that we don't understand."

"Well, we're halfway there." Lithia said.

"I'll say a prayer for us," Perric said. "At least we've got each other. That's a lot."

That was the only positive out of this whole mess.

15

The morning came with a heavy blanket of fog below a cloudy sky. A strong breeze blew in from the west, making the day feel colder than it was. The troop broke their fast and readied themselves for the day. A solemn mood had settled over all of them. Even Ayre was subdued in his morning chit chat.

The sun would have been a better start to the day. Saria loosened her sword in its scabbard. The sight of the temple last night had set her nerves on edge, and she didn't like it. She'd lived through homelessness on the streets of White-crest, survived the arena, served in the duke's army, fought all sorts of monsters and evil people, yet the crumbling temple made her want to run. She shook her head.

You'll never finish if you don't start. Mistress Regina's voice echoed in her head.

Much to Saria's consternation, the Mistress of Bounties was right. They had a job to do and gold to earn. Not finishing a bounty handed to her by the Mistress because the temple ruins looked dodgy wasn't an option. "Let's head out."

Perric, as he often did, took the lead. The others fell into line without a word. Lithia fidgeted with her bow. Ayre spun his knives, while Jileli placed her hand on her spell supplies.

A nervous ripple ran through the troop in response to the eerie tension of the place. Would any of her troop balk if they knew their target was a rare, enchanted item?

Probably not. So that information could wait a bit longer.

The troop made their way back through an unusually quiet forest to the stone path that led to the temple at the top of the hill. Perric stopped at the beginning of the path and waited. Saria joined him to strategize. In the dim daylight, the temple didn't look any more approachable. Fog billowed and floated around and between the structures. It could be hiding any number of things, most of which would be bad news. The three sentry towers were crumbling. The closest had stones scattered around the base.

"Do you hear a groaning noise?" Lithia asked.

"Fuck." Saria heard it but couldn't tell if it was the constant ocean breeze or something worse. "All right, Blades. Get ready for a fight. In and out, nobody dies, and we all make some gold."

Ayre's eyes lit up. "Plus, whatever treasures the temple contains. Insus's temples were opulent before the fall."

"We're here for our bounty item only," Saria said firmly. "We aren't taking unnecessary chances, Ayre. Agreed?"

The rest chimed in that they agreed. Ayre had a smirk on his face that was never a good sign, but they were wasting time. "Perric, take the lead. I'm second, with Lithia bringing up the rear."

"I do have one more question," Ayre said, lifting a finger. "A teeny tiny one that doesn't involve treasure. He continued without waiting for her to give permission. "Why would a person who stole a rich family's fancy dagger bring it...here?"

"It is a good hiding place," Lithia joked. "Nobody will come looking."

"It's not pertinent to our mission," Saria said. "Our target is in that temple and that's that." They were all suspicious but all still willing to trust her. She couldn't push it much longer. "Shall we?"

The paladin knelt, silently mouthing a prayer to Drohara. His sword began to glow with a golden light. He stood and turned to the group. "There are undead here, so be careful."

"How do you know?" Lithia already had an arrow nocked and ready. "I couldn't make out what was moving up the hill."

"Drohara has blessed my sword. The golden light of the sun will increase the closer we are to the minions of darkness." Perric strode up the path to the temple.

Saria followed Perric through the fog. Jileli walked on her left, Ayre on the right. Clouds of mist swirled around their feet as they continued up the incline. The smell of rotting flesh wafted to Saria, turning her stomach.

"Heads up," Perric called.

Figures emerged from the mist far faster than Saria expected. Perric's sword flared, illuminating the rotted faces of the zombies that stomped toward them. Perric struck the closest one, shearing the head from its body. It landed with a wet thud on the ground. The eyes rolled back into its head as it died.

Two shamblers reached out for Saria. Her sword flashed, removing an arm in the process. She kicked out, knocking the second zombie to the ground. An arrow whistled past her ear, taking the first one between the eyes, sending it sprawling on the broken cobblestones.

A beam of red energy streaked from behind Saria. It wrapped around another zombie. Saria recoiled as the magic dissolved the monster, tearing at it until all that was left was a green puddle of goo. She was relieved she hadn't been as sensitive to this particular spell of Jileli's since that wasn't a sensation she'd want to share.

"Watch out!" Ayre yelled. He threw his dagger, which flew end over end, striking the zombie trying to bite Saria on the side of the head. She spun her sword and decapitated it.

"Thanks, Ayre," Saria said, silently berating herself for allowing Jileli's attack to distract her from the fight. All of the undead lay on the ground in pieces which twitched like they were trying to still attack.

Ayre gripped his dagger with two fingers and pulled it from the zombie's head. It released with a sickening squelch. Green ichor dripped from the blade. He carefully wiped the knife on the rags that passed for clothing and grimaced at the smell. "I hate fighting zombies."

"My guess is there are more up the hill," Lithia said from where she'd retrieved her arrows with a minimum of fuss.

Saria turned to Jileli. "That was some work on the zombie."

"Thank you," she said a bit apprehensively. The blood mage hadn't been with them in many battles so far, and seeing her spells in action was intimidating. But they'd hired her for her power, and even Perric seemed to be coming around.

Saria whispered in her ear. "You don't have to worry about using your magic with us."

Jileli's eyes shot to Perric, who used an old cloth to clean his sword. Saria followed her gaze. "He doesn't like it, but he understands. He won't trouble you."

Jileli nodded, but she didn't look convinced.

"Keep moving forward," Perric said, setting off up the hill.

Saria fell in behind the paladin with the others trailing. The troop worked their way up the path, dispatching wandering zombies. Saria and Perric took care of the stragglers, but the troop waited for a mass attack. Zombies tended to gather in herds, and the ones they'd killed so far were small in number.

After fifteen minutes of hacking and slashing, they reached the top of the hill. The temple was even larger than Saria had thought, squatting in the clearing like an island in a sea of grass. Thick ropes of ivy grappled the stone structure. Blocks of fallen rock showed how the plants would eventually destroy the whole thing. Four sets of stairs with stone overhangs led to the main landing that ran the length of the building, but none looked like they could withstand even a strong breeze. The support pillars had decayed so much that it was a miracle they still were upright. Statues in various degrees of broken rested in front of each of the pillars.

"I wonder if anyone is home?" Ayre asked. No one responded.

Saria took the lead across the clearing. The smells of death and decay lessened under the steady wind that blew from the ocean that backed up to the temple. Noises came from the mist that coiled around the scrubby forest that covered the hill.

"We made it." Ayre examined the front of the columned building. "I guess there has to be an entrance somewhere."

"Well, let's go find it," Saria said. After choosing what appeared to be the safest stairs, she strode toward the gloomy overhang that led to the front of the temple. The left-hand statue had been torn in half, but the right one still held a bow at the ready, though its head was gone.

Saria climbed the twenty stairs to the main landing. The treads were wider than Saria expected. The gloom deepened as she walked toward the main building. The landing was thirty feet deep and ran fifty or more feet along the main building. An ornate fresco had been carved into the wall depicting Insus's hunt. Centaurs, satyrs, and other races fought a massive dragon whose tail wrapped around the far corner of the building.

Ayre stepped next to Saria. "Cheerful sight there."

The elf had his trademark smirk plastered across his face. She'd known Ayre for long enough to understand how much the lure of a challenge intrigued the thief. Lithia, Perric, and Jileli stood behind them.

"Is there a door?" Jileli asked.

"I'm sure there is, but I'll have to find the trip switch." Ayre removed a leather pouch of tools from his bag. "Let me take a look."

A loud groan came from down the hill. They all looked at each other.

"Find it fast, Ayre." Saria readied her sword and peered into the fog.

"I'll do my best, oh fearsome leader," Ayre said as he started running his hands over the stonework.

The noise became more intense. Shadows moved in the mist.

A huge shape moved through the fog. "Do better than your best, or this could get ugly,"

Just how bad Saria didn't know, but given the day so far, it wouldn't be good.

16

Saria stood next to Perric. The paladin's sword glowed more fiercely than before.

"That's bad news, right?" Lithia asked, gesturing to the big man's sword.

He nodded. "Something evil is out there."

Saria peered into the gloom. "Ayre, speed it up."

The thief turned to the Blades leader. "If you would like to find a hidden lock in a dilapidated temple's wall, feel free. I'll have a pipe and call out helpful suggestions."

A loud growl rumbled across the clearing. It was followed by a huge undead monstrosity lumbering from the fog. It must have been ten feet tall, and half as wide. Stitchwork held the thing together. It carried a broken halberd in one hand while from the other dangled a long chain. Drool ran down from the corners of its mouth as it groaned at the intruders.

"Sounds like he isn't happy to see us," Ayre said from where he traced the grooves in the stone. "Maybe if we had some ale and a virgin, we could distract him."

"Find the fucking door, Ayre," Saria said, though it came

out more like a shout than the calm tone of command she'd been going for.

The patchwork golem screamed in rage. Black magic emanated from the thing like the stench from a garbage heap. It swung its weapon back and forth, shambling across the clearing toward the Blades up on the landing. Its smell struck like a sledgehammer.

"I'm going to be sick," Lithia said with her hand over her mouth and nose.

"I'll take care of it." Jileli removed a vial from her pouch and drained it into her hand. The syrupy red liquid clung to her fingers like glue. The blood mage spoke in the language Saria was getting used to hearing from her, and the liquid formed into a pulsing orb of light. She threw it at the golem as it stomped closer to the stairs. It struck the monster and dropped to the ground where it returned to bloody goo.

"Not to criticize," Perric said to the mage. "Was that supposed to do that?"

"No," Jileli said, more shaken than Saria had ever seen her. "It must be warded to resist magic."

This was not the time for Jileli's spell to fail. "We do this the old way," Saria said, racing down the stairs to engage the monster with Perric beside her.

The golem's chain arced out, missing Saria but circling Perric's waist. The patchwork monster pulled, sending the paladin to the ground at the base of the stairs. A flaming arrow whistled across the clearing and struck the monster in the head. It shrugged it off, intent on the fallen Perric.

"Not so fast." Saria's long sword flashed through the air and sliced deep into the undead's flesh. Nothing sprayed or oozed. The golem swung the broken halberd at Saria. She pivoted and slammed home three more strikes. Nothing happened other than infuriating the giant.

It roared and slammed the flat of the blade against Saria's

leather chest plate. The force of the blow sent her flying into a nearby statue. It exploded into dust and chunks of stone.

Perric charged to stop the monster from finishing off Saria. His sword glowed, and the intense golden color drove away the shadows cast by the fog. The golem reared away from the sword but parried the first two strikes.

"In the name of Drohara, I banish thee." Perric's frenzied strokes pushed the monster away from Saria. With an overhand blow, Perric knocked the golem off balance. It stumbled a few feet down the hill before it steadied itself.

"Move back to the stairs," Saria called to Perric.

"No, I can finish this thing," he yelled back. The big man took a couple of steps toward the beast before he stopped dead in his tracks. "We've got company."

Saria started to reply, but words failed her. From the fog more shambling creatures formed up around the golem. From the looks of it, there were at least a hundred more undead of all shapes and sizes. Perric turned tail and bolted for the stairs.

"Ayre, have you found the lock?" Lithia asked.

"I'm looking." Ayre had reached the halfway point in the wall, all fifty feet of which were carved. The door could be anywhere, or nowhere, the carvings a distraction. Whoever closed up the temple when it fell had known what they were doing.

"Look faster," Lithia said. "We are about to join the ranks of the undead if we don't get out of here."

For once, Ayre didn't have a comeback, which shocked Saria almost as much as the army of undead headed their way.

Lithia raised her bow, but Jileli stopped her. "Save your arrows. They won't stop the undead."

Lithia grimaced. "I can slow them down. We have to do something."

The horde of undead lurched forward, closing the distance to the temple. Some were intact, while others were missing limbs or other body parts. They pushed on up the hill toward the only living things on the hill.

"Ayre, we need that door now," Perric said over his shoulder.

"I need more time!" Ayre yelled. "There are runes woven into the fresco. If I'm reading this right, we need to find a spear in this whole mess."

Perric stationed himself at the top of the stairs. His sword illuminated the area surrounding the Blades. "I'll hold them for as long as I can. All of you find the spear Ayre is talking about."

"Jileli, with me." Saria strode passed Perric and readied her long sword. "Perric, help Ayre. The light from your sword should speed up the search."

"But Saria—"

"Once we find the door, we're safe," Saria said. And if that wasn't true, if there were more inside, they'd be joining the zombies shortly. "I'll hold them while you search."

The two fastest undead reached the bottom of the stairs. Saria raced halfway down. The first had been an elf at one point. The other was a centaur whose face had been shredded. The elf lunged, but Saria slashed out and took the zombie's head clean off. She pivoted to parry the blow from the centaur, but she realized she was too late.

A bolt of solid red energy shot passed her, taking the centaur full in the chest. It reared up and fell backward, bouncing down the stairs to slam into a column that supported the roof. Dust cascaded down like a heavy summer storm, covering Saria in the process. A few stones crashed onto the stairs.

"I've got an idea," Saria said to Jileli. "I need a distraction."

"Gotcha. Don't let the vapor touch you." Jileli pulled a

green vial from her pouch and opened it. She whispered a spell and then threw it down the stairs. The vial broke when it struck the ground. Smoke billowed out of the shattered vessel, forming into tendrils that snaked out toward the approaching undead. "It won't last long."

Saria grabbed a rock the size of a skull and heaved it at the column above the still twitching centaur. This time, the whole roof groaned while dust and debris rained down. Saria stooped and retrieved an armful of stones.

"What are you doing?" Jileli asked, her eyes wide.

"Trying to…help this place return to nature," Saria panted between hurling stone after stone at the column. Gravel sprinkled down around it.

The vapor from Jileli's spell wrapped around the front row of the oncoming zombies. They slowed as the mist congealed into ropes then tore each apart like a child tearing up its favorite treat. Demonic power rippled around the clearing as the grizzly magic did its work. Saria paused, stone in her hand, transfixed by the sight. Jileli's power tickled inside her like she touched an electric eel.

"Saria!" Jileli screamed.

That brought her back from the macabre scene below. Saria bolted back up the stairs and dropped the rest of the stones at her feet. She'd have to be more careful not to get distracted when she could sense the magic. "See if you can find more."

Jileli nodded, already breaking into a run.

"Have you found the spear?" Saria asked the others, who were running their hands over the carved stonework.

"Not yet, oh mighty leader, but at least we have a clue," Ayre said, his hands dancing across the mosaic of the god's hunt.

The spell below had ended, and the surviving monsters were now pushing up the hill at a great pace. The golem led the charge, trampling smaller undead under his massive frame. They reached the bottom of the stairs and started to climb.

Saria hefted a rock and threw it at the same column as before. Because she was throwing from above, the stones struck with more force. Larger rocks began falling, bouncing off the patchwork monster, but taking out the smaller of the troops.

"Come on!" Saria screamed at the approaching undead.

In rapid succession, she threw three more stones at the left-hand column. It swayed dangerously from the repeated blows. Jileli dropped more rocks by Saria's feet. "Go help the others."

With a new supply of projectiles, Saria set to work. She threw as hard as she could. Her arm burned from the exertion of throwing large rocks that far with any force. Eash strike caused the pillar to sway more and more. Stones, dirt, and moss fell across the stairs as she continued the onslaught. She sneezed repeatedly, but kept up the barrage of stones. The dust made it hard to see. Parts of the roof rained down onto the monsters.

"I found it," Ayre shouted. He pushed open a large door. "Saria, come on."

She heaved the largest rock at the left-hand pillar. It wavered, then with a groan, it tumbled, dropping the roof onto the stairs. The sound was deafening as the collapsing rock obliterated the monsters.

"Show off," Ayre said with a huff.

17

Perric took the lead. The glow from his sword barely illuminated the absolute darkness of the room they entered. At least the undead weren't close by.

A cautious inspection of the chamber revealed four pillars in the center, supporting a stone ceiling. Each had been carved with elaborate designs that were barely visible in the gloom. Cobwebs, droppings, and dust covered every surface, except where rats and other vermin had left their footprints.

"Cheery sort of place," Ayre said to no one in particular.

"Hush," Saria said in a low voice. "We don't know what could be in here."

Ayre peered off into the darkness. Nothing stirred, but a faint rasping sound came from the far end of the room. The thief had his daggers out in a heartbeat. "Probably prudent advice," he whispered to Saria.

Saria pulled out the leather sack and retrieved the unlimited light stones Jileli had found on the Skulls. There were six in the bag, so she left one alone and gave each member one.

The stones were powerful artifacts, and soon the room glowed in a golden tone, as close to daylight as it could be.

Torches guttered, lantern needed oil, but these beauties needed nothing. "Group loot. You've earned these. I'd appreciate it if, while you're with the Blades, you don't sell them, but I can't stop you."

Each member of the team held their stone like it was glass. These relics had been around for centuries, so they had stood the test of time. Saria let the cool, round sphere settle into her palm, hardly trusting herself not to break it.

"Thank you," Ayre said softly. "This is a gift beyond value."

"We are a troop, and you've all earned it. We fought the Skulls as a team, and here we are and they are rotting," Saria said. The heat in her voice surprised her. She'd been attacked, betrayed, and everything in between, and it hadn't ever felt as personal as the Skulls ambushing her people at the behest of the assassin's guild, or so they assumed.

Perric cleared his throat. "We should keep moving."

Now that they were at their destination, it was time to come clean about the bounty. She was asking the troop to put their lives on the line for this, for Brar Opalback. They at least deserved to know the whole story, and Regina had said she could share once they reached the temple. They wouldn't like knowing the dwarven sorceress was at the heart of the request, but they would like that the bounty was a lot more gold than originally described. "We are looking for an orb—"

"The bounty is for a dagger." Lithia said. "The bounty is paid when the dagger is retrieved from the thieves."

"I can tell you the truth now," Saria said. "The Mistress of Bounties actually tasked us with retrieving a magic orb from this temple. The dagger bounty distracted the other troops and sent them on a wild goose chase. Brar Opalback, a mage from Whitecrest, hired us to find and return this artifact."

"Why did she make you wait to tell us? And why did you agree?" Perric grumbled. The big man prided himself on honesty, for the most part. He turned prickly when the rules weren't being followed.

"That's easy," Lithia said. Her tone conveyed annoyance and a touch of hurt. "I'm new. She couldn't trust that I wouldn't run off and sell the information."

"And that's why she's the leader," Ayre said with a glare back at the archer. "Wouldn't be the first time we'd been betrayed."

"It doesn't seem fair to hide this information from us, even if the Mistress asked you to. Jileli's horns glowed a soft purple. If they darkened, the troop knew trouble was brewing. "Recovering an enchanted artifact isn't quite on the same level as a stolen dagger."

Saria hadn't been happy about keeping this hidden, either, but she had done it and now must take the heat. "Regina worked around the rules to ask us to take this mission. She couldn't let anyone know about that or the fact that the true bounty was for an artifact. What kind of scramble would have erupted if the other troops had known that? Gnedain almost started a fight and that's when he thought it was for a dagger. Imagine the trouble telling the other troops a rare magical relic was the goal. But she trusted us to accomplish the mission and return with the artifact."

"She trusted you," Lithia pointed out. "Not us."

"I've known her most of my life. I did warn everyone when I explained we were headed here instead of Tolle," Saria said. "And you still agreed to come."

"I didn't think it would be something like this," Perric said. The big man rubbed his chin. "We agreed to be honest with each other, and that pact has been broken."

Ayre scoffed. "You, my friend, have a mouth wider than the krakens. Once you get a few ales and a soft woman under your arm, you are a font of information."

"That's not true," Perric said, his voice rising with his anger.

"Oh, it is, my boisterous friend. I heard you tell Avilya, your favorite 'friend', all about the bounty to get Malen Heartbender. We've agreed to keep that quiet to not attract attention," Ayre said.

"When I was researching troops before the faire, I'd heard from Bleg that you were boasting about the deal Saria cut with the Duke of Auano. Nice bit of gold on that one, huh, Perric?" Lithia said.

"And don't forget when he told Daleira all about stealing from the ogre," Ayre said. "All of those were to stay with the troop, not outsiders. It could be the reason we've got assassins after us."

"Well, Perric? We can be quits after this if I've sullied your honor." Saria hated having this conversation in a centuries old temple that housed who-knows-what, but Perric could be problematic if he got his neck up.

"No," Perric said, his cheeks flushing. "I may have been hasty in my anger. We'll discuss it more if we live through this."

"Agreed." Saria produced the amulet from around her neck, held it in her hand, and said 'Brar'. The image of the dagger appeared only to fade out and reveal a glass sphere set in a pewter base. "Artifacts fetch a huge amount of gold on the black market, but we will deliver it if we can retrieve it."

"Of course, we will deliver it. We honor our word, well, most of us," Perric said, glaring at Ayre. He returned to studying the image of the orb. "The runes aren't familiar."

Ayre started to respond, but Saria's scowl killed it dead.

"I think they might be draconic," Jileli said, sitting on the ground next to Saria. Lithia and Ayre moved to see better as well. "No, they aren't quite right."

"Tennin script has those kind of loops." Lithia pursed her

lips as she studied the orb. "See how the symbols have that twist in them?"

"It could be." Jileli squinted at the details of the script along the base. "If it was created by tennin magic, it would be a strong artifact. The tennin race was wiped out near the end of the wars."

"Next," Saria said.

A handwritten note appeared. "The troop that returns the orb to the Mistress of Bounties will receive two hundred gold."

Saria glanced around the circle. "The Blades were hand-picked to do this bounty and we are being paid much more than the fifty gold on the dagger bounty. I trust you are beginning to understand why."

"Still," Ayre said. "If I'd known we were coming to a temple remote enough to keep an artifact safe, I'd have found a way to carry a lot more. These places tend to be loaded."

Lithia smiled, but it wasn't a full smile. "Looks like I picked the right time to join."

"I wouldn't say that until after we've completed the bounty." Jileli cautioned. "Temples might have more loot, but as we have already seen they also have more guardians."

"Now, back to business. I don't know anything more than it is an orb that was supposedly housed here when nexus portals opened and the monsters flooded in. An oracle told Brar where to find it, and hopefully it's in here. Spread out. If you see anything unusual, get Ayre before you touch it."

The Blades spread out. Perric crept across the room to the front left corner. Lithia went to the back left corner while Ayre went to the front right and Saria to the back right. Jileli moved to the center of the room, where she could unleash her magic if needed.

"There has to be more to this chamber," Ayre said. "Temples this big have more rooms that just this one."

"Agreed." Perric ran his hands through the dust, looking for clues. "The temple to Drohara had hundreds of rooms. The monsters swarmed it within the first year of the war."

"History lessons can wait. We need to find a way out of this room," Lithia said. Her tone still held a touch of hostility.

Had she been impulsive in choosing the archer to join the Blades? Too late for such thoughts, but it nagged at the back of Saria's mind. The fact that the Skulls had death markers for the troop also complicated matters.

Then again, Lithia could also be inclined to sulk like Perric. Time would tell.

"Rotate to your left," Perric said. "We need to find an exit."

"I found a club of some kind on the ground." Lithia held up the wooden item for everyone to see. "Might have been a belaying pin. What would it be doing here?"

"Well, we are on the coast," Jileli said. "These columns have faces carved into them. My guess is there are depictions of Insus during his hunts. Some have animals around him, and some have people worshiping him."

"Keep searching." Saria scoured the wall and floor as she rotated to the left around the room.

"Ah." Ayre used his foot to brush away the dust. "We have a clue. There is a pattern etched into the floor."

"What does that have to do with anything?" Perric asked.

"There is a crystal embedded in the center of the wall there. My guess is that these columns must be part of unlocking the exit," Ayre said.

Jileli knelt and brushed a clear spot on the floor. "There are designs set into the floor tiles here in the center as well. They could be ornamental."

"It's possible," Ayre said as he continued to clean off more of the pattern. "But think of it this way. They concealed the doors as a defensive mechanism in case of attack. When help arrived, they would need to know how to unlock the room and enter the other chambers. It's not like they could write it on the wall."

"It makes sense," Lithia said. "So, what does the pattern mean?"

Saria spotted a lump in the dust by her feet. She retrieved a wooden baton from the debris. It was as long as her forearm with a handle at one end and tapered end at the other. She pushed it through her belt. "I found another wooden pin."

"That can't be a coincidence," Lithia said. "Why would anyone leave these things lying around a room?"

Good question. Saria continued her search, pushing piles of dust around to see if it revealed any other clues.

"Oh! There are holes in the columns," Jileli announced, her excitement palpable. "What if the batons are to rotate the columns?"

Saria examined the wooden spike in her hand. She'd seen them on ships holding ropes in place. Why would they be in a temple? She walked to the center where Jileli stood. In the combined light of the two stones, she could make out a face on one of the columns with an O for a mouth. She slotted the pin in the opening. It slid into place. "The pin fits, though it seems kind of obscene."

"Don't touch it!" Ayre yelled, running over to join them. "There must be four pins. If we try to move them one at a time, all sorts of bad things could happen."

When Ayre, the risk taker, called for caution, all the Blades obliged. While he could be annoying, no one ever questioned his knowledge. He'd saved the Blades from numerous traps, and they all followed his lead.

"I found another one," Perric called.

"Find the last one and we can get out of here," Ayre said.

Saria went to where she'd left off and scoured the floor. After a few minutes, Ayre cheered. "I've got the last one."

The Blades converged on the center of the room. Ayre took the pins from each and slotted them in the holes that faced away from the center. "The designs flow to the right, so we turn the pillars that way as well. We need to do this in unison. Saria, who do you want on guard in case the trap releases something?"

"Lithia, stand watch. If anything comes out, fire first, ask questions later."

"Got it." Lithia stepped outside of the columns, her bow readied.

"Ayre, you make the call," Saria said. "My guess is we only have one try."

The thief checked each column thoroughly. After three rounds, he stopped by one of the columns. "Pick a column. On the count of three, we each push clockwise. Is everyone ready?"

Saria took a deep breath and held it. She'd been with Ayre long enough to know that traps could release any sort of deadly toxins.

Ayre took position at his column. "On the count of three. One, two, three."

They all pushed, but nothing happened.

18

W hy didn't they budge?" Saria asked. "I thought the pillars opened the secret door?"

Ayre huffed. "I thought they would, especially with the wooden pins."

"We could try knocking down the columns. Might show us how they work," Perric said.

"And bring down the whole place on our heads," Lithia said with a glance at the cobweb draped ceiling. "Let's think of something else."

"At least we'd have air in here. Why is it so warm?" Perric leaned against the column next to him and wiped the sweat from his brow. His skin glistened in the light from the stone he carried.

"Let's not stick around to find out," Ayre responded. "Help me clear the floor. We've missed something."

Perric grumbled under his breath but did as requested. "What are we looking for?"

"Once we can see the whole design, we should be able to figure out how to get out," Ayre said.

"Or die of overheating," Perric said.

Saria got on her hands and knees and used her backpack as a makeshift broom to push the dust toward the wall. She held the light stone near the inset design that flowed around the whole room. Semi-precious stones flared in the illumination. Jade, onyx, and silver shimmered as Saria ran her finger along the curved lines. After a few minutes, the head of an eagle emerged. Its eye was made from a white crystal. "Ayre, it's an eagle."

"Mine is a dragon," Perric said from across the square the columns formed.

"This one is a snake," Jileli said from her spot on the left-hand side of the room.

Ayre stood. "This looks to be a lion."

"Could it be a chimera?" Lithia asked. "Insus hunted all sorts of monsters."

She'd seen puppeteers enacting Insus, slaying the demon of destruction whose symbol was the fantastic beast. "If the legend is to be believed, Insus saved the world from Tihallia, the four-headed monster."

"That makes sense." Jileli moved to the closest column and lightly ran her fingers over it. "Do the other columns have Insus on them?"

Saria returned to the pillar she'd examined. After a few minutes, she found the god holding a barbed lance. The rest of the column had flames and dying people around him. Overall, it was a gruesome story. "He's on here."

Ayre studied each pillar in turn, without touching the carved surfaces. "I don't see any traps, but that doesn't mean there aren't any. My guess is each set of weapons is an indication of his fight with the goddess of destruction, Tihallia. If we rotate the pillars to the correct location, the door should appear."

"Well, that should be easy. Everyone knows the tale," Perric said, his voice growing in strength. "The lance kills the dragon, the club the lion, the fire eliminates the snake, and the bow the eagle."

"Are you sure?" Lithia scratched her nose while she thought. "I thought the fire destroyed the stumps after the heads were cut off?"

Perric snorted. "I spent years in training, and I know all the old tales about the gods and goddesses. If we line up the weapons with the creature, then we should get out of here."

"Ayre?" Saria asked. Perric might know the stories, but Ayre was born to be a thief.

"I think Perric is right. If we each push on a pillar to the right, then the weapons will be pointed at the creatures they killed."

"And if we're wrong?"

"No idea, but the undead out there would have overrun us eventually, so we're one step ahead." Ayre moved to the closest column. "Lithia, stand watch. On the count of three, we all push in the opposite direction this time."

The three Blades took their positions.

"One, two, three, push!" Ayre said. Nothing happened at first, but slowly the columns turned in unison.

Saria glanced down and realized the pillars were constructed on a revolving disc. When the weapons faced each of the monsters, a beam of light shot out of each of the monoliths.

"Down!" Ayre screamed. They each dove to the floor without question. The crystal Ayre found in the wall had counterparts on each of the four walls. They reflected and bounced around the room. Flames flared where cobwebs or other flammable materials crossed the beams.

"What is going on?" Saria asked from where she lay on the floor. Smoke started to fill the room as the fire raced through the centuries of cobwebs. "We need to get out of here."

"Stay low, but push the opposite way," Ayre said, crawling over to the column. "One, two, three, push!"

The beams shut off once the disc rotated. The smoke got worse with each passing moment. "Keep going," Ayre said between coughing. The fire wasn't a threat, but the smoke was.

The beams fired out again when they reached the monsters on the floor. The Blades kept pushing. Saria saw the outline of the snake on the floor before her. With one last shove, she pushed it until the snake's face was aligned with the club on the totem. The beams reappeared, but instead of striking the walls, the light connected with the snake's crystal eye. It flared, sending a streak of illumination straight into the air. The light show intensified before the grinding of stone announced the hidden exit was opening.

"Hurry! I don't know how long this will stay open," Ayre said. They crawled across the floor, more to stay away from the descending smoke than the light show. Each of the Blades stumbled down the newly found hallway. Saria was the last through.

On the wall, a lever stood out in the dim light of the stones. She pulled the lever, and the wall descended, cutting them off from the smoky room. They all sank to the floor, pulling out water flasks to clear the residual smoke from their throats.

"That was intense," Lithia said. "Do you always cut it that close?"

Ayre shrugged. "Usually, it's much closer. That was downright easy. What else can go wrong?"

A loud shriek echoed through the air from the darkness beyond.

"You had to ask, didn't you?" Saria said.

Ayre smirked at his leader. "Well, at least we know we aren't alone."

19

The high-pitched wailing continued from down the hallway. Saria stood inside the secret door, which was keeping the majority of smoke out of the rest of the temple. The odor of burnt wood and other things made for a bad mixture of smells. Light radiated from each of their magical stones, creating a ten-foot puddle of illumination in the darkness.

"Perric, take the lead. Jileli, bring up the rear," Saria said. She stepped in behind Perric as he clanked down the hall.

"Any chance you could make more noise, Perric?" Ayre said from behind Saria. They had to raise their voices to be heard over the nonstop wail. "Maybe you have a trumpet to signal the charge?"

"When you take the brunt of attacks, we'll see how quickly you want to give up better armor," Perric said. He resumed moving down the hall, though a bit more on the quiet side.

"If you—"

Saria pivoted toward the thief. His next words died on his

lips. "Shut the fuck up, Ayre. We don't need your commentary."

Ayre nodded.

They continued down the hall toward the presumed source of whatever was shrieking. Perric used his sword to sweep the worst of the cobwebs out of the way, but they still found their way into Saria's hair, face, and mouth. She scrubbed her face to get the worst of them off.

The screech echoed through the emptiness of the temple. Whatever it was, it wasn't happy. Did any undead make noises like that? A temple guarded by zombies tended to be full of them.

After about forty feet, Perric stopped. "There are two openings on the right. I can't make out if they are passages or dead ends."

"Ayre, can you scout the first?"

"Sure." He switched the glowing stone to his left hand and pulled his dagger. He glanced at Saria. "You've got my back?"

"Always," she answered.

Ayre turned the corner and disappeared into the adjoining passage. Saria counted three, then followed. She left her longsword in the scabbard and withdrew her dagger. Hallway fighting didn't lend itself well to the sword due to the space limitations.

Faded images decorated the walls, depicting one of Insus' hunts. A variety of men and women who seemed to be native to the Southern Holm of yore rode horses with hunting dogs leading the way. The temple must have been amazing in its heyday.

Ayre and his bubble of light stopped after twenty feet. The roof had collapsed, closing off the passage and creating a dead end. "Nothing much to see here," the thief said. His fingers twitched as he stared at the fallen rubble. "I wonder what was back there? Could have been a treasure room."

"This close to the entrance? Nah, probably where the servants were housed," Saria said. "My question is did this collapse or did they block it on purpose?"

"What if the orb is back there?"

"Then we'll be digging it out after we explore the rest." Saria returned to the group. The second hallway roof had collapsed as well. Two dead-ends and they were just getting started.

"Keep going?" Perric asked Saria.

"We've got to find the orb and probably a way out since I doubt we want to head out the front door."

"I can't imagine we'd get a warm reception," Perric said with a chuckle. "I wonder how many the collapsing roof took out."

"Not enough," Lithia said. "I like the idea of avoiding a rematch with the undead."

"Don't we all," Jileli said. She glanced behind them anxiously.

Saria patted her shoulder. "Between the collapsed roof, the hidden door, and the wall of fire behind us, I don't think we've got anything to worry about anything out there." She didn't mention they should be worried about what was ahead, since it was a given.

Another twenty feet and the corridor widened out to their left. Rocks were strewn across the floor from where parts of the ceiling had given way. Pools of stagnant water gave off a musty odor that reminded Saria of the sewers under Whitecrest. The only other opening in the room was a doorway in the back left corner, but it was mostly filled with rubble.

"Whoever decorated this place did a terrible job," Ayre said. The far end of the room remained dark. Another shriek announced they weren't alone, as if they needed a reminder. Now that they were closer, the noise had become intermittent but sounded more animal than person in nature. Too bad the creatures that lived in temple ruins were as dangerous as any warrior. Well, there was nothing they could do to prepare besides find it and hope for the best.

"Spread out and search for anything out of the ordinary. Lithia, stand watch at the doorway. Shout if anything comes at us," Saria said.

"Will do." Lithia unslung her bow and moved to cover the way they had come in. Ayre stalked along the back wall, searching for traps.

Saria, with Jileli and Perric flanking her, strode to the middle of the room. A raised stone fire pit occupied the center of the room. Stagnant water had filled a portion with bits of debris floating on top of it. Beyond it a staircase the width of the room rose to an altar with a large urn on the right side. The room was once forty feet to a side before the roof collapsed, leaving that corner buried in rubble. No daylight or anything else could get through the amount of fallen stone.

"Do we search it?" Jileli asked, eying the disgusting pool. "I vote no."

"I agree with the mage," Perric said, though his tone spoke volumes about how much he hated to agree with her. "Unless Ayre starts running his mouth again, then I think we throw him in."

"Me?" Ayre asked from where he examined a carved section of wall. "I am a delight and the only thing keeping you from dying a horrible death."

"How do you figure th—" Perric started but was interrupted by a loud screech.

A round metal structure with a series of stakes and worn leather restraints crashed down from the center of the ceiling. A rusted iron chain ran back up into the darkness. The grate stopped a few feet above the pool.

"Seriously!" Jileli shouted. Her eyes blazed a dark purple, which mirrored the glow from her horns. She pivoted to face Ayre. "You could have warned us."

Ayre's eyes grew wide at the sight of the enraged blood mage. "Sorry," he stammered. "I released the lever, thinking it would open a passage, not drop the cook top."

Saria placed a hand on Jileli's shoulder, who yanked away and faced Saria. It took everything Saria had to not retreat in fear. A startled Jileli was apparently a recipe for disaster. If their mage was affected by unexpected events, that was something they could learn to work with, considering Jileli's other talents.

Saria kept a cool tone. "It was an accident."

The mage took a deep breath. "You startled me is all. I wasn't expecting it and I shouldn't have yelled."

Saria nodded. "We all have our weak spots."

"I'm sorry," Ayre said. "I really thought it opened a secret door."

After a few moments, Jileli closed her eyes. The pulsing purple of her horns diminished, and when she opened her eyes, they were back to normal. "I'm sorry, too, Ayre. This place is difficult to endure. Something is wrong here. I can feel it like slime dripping down my back."

"We are all tense," Perric said. He was still shaken, though Saria wasn't sure if it was from the plummeting grate or the temple. "If we are to survive this place, we need to work together."

"Ayre, please warn us if you find anything else."

He gestured affirmatively. "Of course."

"Perric, you and I will check the altar. Jileli, take a seat on the stairs and relax for a minute," Saria said.

The blood mage opened her mouth to protest but did as she was asked. She went to the edge of the stairs and sat. She tossed the light stone between her hands, which cast wild shadows around the room.

Saria climbed up and studied the ceramic urn. It was enameled and showed scenes of gruesome killings and feasts in what she assumed was the temple in its prime.

Perric approached the altar and walked around it carefully. Stones were scattered about, which made the footing uneven. "There is a box on the altar. Ayre, do you want a look?"

The thief skulked across the room and joined Perric. He studied the box and nodded. "Whoever forged the box was a true artisan. The scroll work is phenomenal."

"Less talking, more opening," Saria said to the thief. She was keen to find the orb and escape this place.

Ayre retrieved his tools from his pack and laid them out on the stone altar. He looked at Jileli. "I'm going to try to open it now. Are we ready?"

Everyone signaled they were, but Ayre didn't move until Jileli had answered. He withdrew a long thin metal rod, fixed a metal plate on the end, and inserted it into the keyhole. A snap and a metallic ping answered his probing. He set down the first tool and grabbed a pair of tweezers. He gently pulled the needle from the keyhole and held it up. "Not sure the poison would still be active, but better safe."

He used a thin-bladed knife to open the latch and raise the top of the coffer. "Well, look at that."

"What is it?" Perric asked.

"We've got company!" Lithia yelled from her post. Noises flooded in from the back opening.

"To arms!" Saria shouted.

20

From the back corner of the room, rubble began to shift and fall from the blocked doorway. Gray hands thrust the stones free as whatever it was tried to claw its way into the room with them.

Lithia raised her bow, but Saria advised, "Don't waste your arrows until we know what we're fighting. Perric, with me."

Perric charged down the stairs and joined Saria behind the fire pit. Lithia ran from her guard position to stand behind the two warriors.

"What is it?" Ayre asked.

Perric hoisted his blade, which glowed brighter the more the creature pushed into the room. "More undead."

"Wonderful." Ayre pulled his knives and took up his position beside Jileli on the stairs.

The blood mage had her pouch of reagents open. She waited for Saria to call the shot.

A head covered in long gray hair emerged from the pile. The thing clawed its way into the room. It wore rotted leather armor, with a sword on one hip and a bow strapped across its back. When it rose, Saria realized this wasn't a zombie.

"Leave this place," the undead warrior said. "Lord Insus set me, Guard Captain Fenwick and my men, to guard this sacred place until his return."

"We are searching for an orb," Saria said. The creature's eyes were a milky white shot through with black streaks. Its black teeth were sharped to points which stood out from the pale skin. It pulled the sword from the rotted scabbard, dropping pieces of leather to the floor.

"Lord Insus's gifts are for his use. This is your last warning, interlopers. Return to the world of the living and leave us be to carry out our instructions."

"It looks like it's only you, my friend," Ayre said with a bow. "I am Ayre of the Niverham elves. We mean you no harm, but we've been tasked with retrieving the orb, and I don't think you can stop us."

The thing erupted in an eerie laugh. "My brothers and sisters, rise and protect our home."

The pile of rubble tumbled down in an avalanche as more of the undead crawled over the mound of fallen stone to join the guard captain.

"Great job, Ayre." Perric readied his sword, which now illuminated the room. "You want to ask them about their pet dragon next?"

"If there's an undead dragon, we may be outmatched," he answered with his normal bravado.

The undead formed ranks around the captain. All wore tattered armor and held a variety of weapons. In total, they now faced eight of the undead warriors. "Leave now or you will join our ranks to protect the temple for all eternity," Captain Fenwick said.

"The world is full of opportunities, isn't it?" Ayre said.

"We are getting job offers wherever we go. I think we should pass on this one, though."

Saria rolled her eyes. Ayre's mouth would be the death of him one day. She hoped he didn't get the rest of them killed in the process. "Blades, attack the archers first. Go!"

Lithia struck. Arrows sped across the room, sinking deep into the three undead in the process of raising their bows. One dropped to the floor with an arrow through one eye. Within moments, the corpse dissolved into dust, leaving behind its armor and weapons.

"So they can die," Perric said as he ran next to Saria to engage the creatures.

Saria swung an overhanded blow at the gristly haired captain. He parried the strike easily, setting him even more apart from the typical zombie. The clang of metal on metal filled the room. The sword might be an antique, but it held up under the blow.

Perric sidestepped an awkward thrust of a halberd from the left while taking the head off of the undead to his right. A shower of dust erupted as the thing broke apart. "These undead stink."

Saria blocked Fenwick's slashing blow with her longsword and dagger. The guard captain's heavier falchion was more cleaver than sword. If she blocked with the flat of her blade, it could snap.

Arrows whistled between Lithia and the two undead archers. A bolt of pure red magic streaked across the room, striking an undead who had leapt onto the stone wall of the pit to flank Saria. It screamed as the magic swirled around it, tearing it apart.

Fenwick glanced at the screaming guard, and it left an opening for Saria to drive her blade at her distracted foe. The blade impaled Fenwick. The guard captain didn't seem to notice and backhanded Saria, knocking her aside. Blood sprayed from her nose and mouth, and her foot caught on the edge of the fire pit. She hit the ground right before the captain's sword flashed through where her head would have been if she hadn't fallen.

Luckiest unplanned tumble of all time.

Perric, having eliminated the second undead, jumped over Saria and engaged the captain. The glowing blade flooded the room with holy light, forcing the undead away from him.

Saria climbed to her feet and grabbed her sword. Ayre traded blows with another warrior to the right. The thief danced around the much larger undead, stabbing and slicing at will. Lithia had taken down a second archer.

Saria circled the ongoing fight between the paladin and the captain. She dispatched the archer with ease. Ayre finished off the guard he'd been toying with.

Perric's sword work was good, but the guard captain was better. The winged sword batted the falchion to the side, but the follow-up stroke went wide. Saria saw her chance. She raced up behind Fenwick and brutally chopped his sword arm off at the shoulder. The arm disintegrated while the blade clattered to the ground.

"Hold!" Saria shouted, stopping Perric from ending the fight. "We seek information, not combat."

"Too late for that, don't you think?" Ayre asked.

She shot him a glare and continued. "Tell us where the orb is, and we'll free you to continue your duty to guard the temple."

The undead cackled an awful laugh that made Saria's skin crawl. "The master of the temple put the orb out of reach of all mortals. I will summon more of my brothers and sisters and we will—"

So much for negotiation. Saria slashed her sword across Fenwick's exposed neck and took his head off. "I'm done.

Hurry up and finish searching the room. Who knows how long we have before reinforcements show up?"

"The chest on the altar had a few promising trinkets," Ayre said. "You might want to look."

"Fine," Saria said, then turned to the others. "Perric, go check where they came from. We need to ensure we don't get any more surprises. Jileli and Lithia, search the rest of the room but don't touch anything you find. Call Ayre."

"Don't you think we should heal you first?" Perric asked Saria. "You took a pretty good shot there."

"What?" Saria asked, then remembered the guard captain had struck her across the face. She touched her lips and winced at the pain. Her fingers smeared with bright red blood. "I guess."

Perric sheathed his sword and approached the Blade's leader. "It will only take a few minutes."

"No, I need you to check the door and make sure we aren't attacked. Ayre, go with him until Jileli is done healing me up."

The elf bowed. "Of course, my most esteemed leader."

"Hold on," Perric said, his face flushing red. "You're going to let a demon heal you over the eternal grace of Drohara?"

"It's fine, Saria," Jileli said. Her eyes were locked on the floor, but her horns flickered. "I can guard the door while—"

"That's not what I said." Saria glanced between the two impatiently. "Perric's winged sword is the best indicator of undead we have, so I need Perric looking for other undead. Luckily, Jileli can also heal. The Blades are lucky to have two healers. Now stop being an ass, Perric, and make sure we aren't caught unaware."

Perric opened his mouth, but snapped it shut. Through gritted teeth, he said, "Fine. Ayre, let's go."

Ayre followed, chirping about something Saria couldn't

hear. If anyone could distract the paladin, it was Ayre. Lithia followed the two.

Jileli caught Saria's eye. "Thank you."

She didn't want the mage thinking that she wasn't trusted, especially after Regina had insisted that Saria not tell her team the truth about the bounty until they reached the temple. Trust had to go both ways, and you also had to know your team had faith in you. "You are a fully blooded Blade, and I won't have Perric's beliefs interfering with our team. Do you have an empty vial?"

"Yes, but…"

Saria had been the new one joining troops before the Blades and knew what it felt like to be the new person. Some troops welcomed you with open arms, others waited to see you in combat before wanting to get to know you. In the mage's case, Jileli was already an outcast and needed to know she belonged, or she might hesitate at a crucial moment, worried about the ramifications of using her blood magic in ways beyond stopping their enemies. "Give it to me."

The blood mage pulled a fresh vial from her stash and handed it over. Saria took it and unstoppered the cork. "This is going to fucking suck." Before she could change her mind, she gripped her damaged nose and squeezed. Blood gushed into the vial and all over her hands. When the vial was half filled, she handed it to Jileli and wiped her hands on her pants.

"Why?" Jileli asked, staring at the vial like it was a viper.

Saria gave her a grin, which she quickly regretted because of the bruises from the captain's blow. "Waste not, want not —right? Human blood isn't as strong as that troglodyte we got you a few days ago, but you might need it is a pinch."

The blood mage nodded. She cleaned the vial, marked it, and put it in her pouch. Once the task was complete, she took Saria's head in her hands. "Ready?"

"Do you need more blood to cast the spell?"

Jileli laughed. "There is enough on your face to wipe out a troop. A simple healing spell won't take much."

"Go ahead."

The mage closed her eyes and a second later, a loud crack from Saria's broken nose sounded. The pain vanished along with the sensation of the blood on her face.

Jileli smiled and patted her cheek before releasing her. "Done."

Saria touched her face. It felt normal, and the simple spell hadn't triggered that fascination inside her that had occurred a few other times with Jileli's magic. It didn't seem to be consistent. Perhaps she simply had to get used to being around a demon's power? "Thank you."

Ayre strolled over. "If you are done getting pretty, Perric found the exit and we have the chest to look at."

Things were looking up.

21

"Now that is interesting," Saria said when Ayre held out the package that had been wrapped in tattered oilcloth. Three shining arrows glistened in the dim light. "Those look like mithral arrowheads. What does the script say?"

"The runes look elvish, but they aren't. The rest of the chest has some coins and an emerald choker that might buy you an ale if you're lucky or the buyer is blind."

"Give the arrows to Lithia, she might have an idea. I'm going to check out the exit."

Ayre nodded. "I'm going to search the altar for secret compartments. I doubt the orb would be here, but better to be sure."

"Agreed." Saria went over to Perric who stood in front of the doorway where the undead had come from. Now that part of the rubble had been cleared by their arrival through it, a doorway could be seen. "Did Ayre check it?"

"Yeah." Perric's tone made it clear that he was still pissed about being sent to guard instead of healing her. He looked her over. "At least she fixed your broken nose."

"Perric, I understand you don't like her blood magic or that she's part succubus. What I'm not putting up with is your attitude toward her. We are a team, and we all pull together, or we fall apart. The question is, are you one of us?"

"As long as you are the leader, I am. If she betrays you, I will use everything I have to kill her."

"Fair enough," she said. Perric was as loyal as the day was long. When he'd signed on with the Blades, he fully committed. "You're assuming I won't kill anyone who turns on the Blades?"

He studied her for a minute. "True. Should we find out where this passage goes?"

"Yes, as a team." Saria called to the rest. "Let's move out. I've got a bad feeling about this place."

"A few undead try to knock your head off and suddenly we are having forebodings?" Ayre asked as he approached.

Lithia and Jileli joined the group. "Did anyone see anything?"

A series of head shakes answered her. "Ayre, take point. Perric, next, Lithia in the rear."

Ayre scrambled over the broken stones and entered a downward staircase. "Stairs to a lower level. Very promising."

"I'm not sure after everything that going deeper into the temple is something I'd call promising," Lithia said. If Ayre heard her, he didn't say anything.

Perric's crossing wasn't so easy. A lot of cursing accompanied the big man climbing over the fallen stones. Saria made it across with much less fuss. Lithia and Jileli followed. The landing was ten feet on each side. The wide stairs descended into the darkness. Unlike the wide-open stairs in the duke's mansion, these were walled in so there would be no unexpectant drops over a banister.

"Stay back a bit," Ayre said. The thief's tone had changed

to a much more serious one, which Saria marked as a bad thing. Ayre never got nervous. Or serious.

He crept down with only the glow rock to illuminate his way. Even with elvish night vision, the pitch black would have been impossible to navigate. After a few minutes, Ayre gave the all clear.

Perric went down first. His winged sword remained dark, which at least meant they weren't near any undead. Halfway down, they all heard a click, and he froze. "I stepped on something."

Ayre sped into action, reaching Perric in a heartbeat. He set the glow stone next to his foot and examined the step. "Lift your toes, but not your foot."

He did as instructed. He could have been a stone statue for all he moved.

"Fuck," Ayre said. "I missed the pressure plate in the stair. I'm not sure what he triggered, but it can't be good."

"Everyone head down the stairs and leave me. Drohara will protect me."

"Lithia and Jileli, go to the next landing below. I'll handle this," Saria said.

"I can disarm it," Ayre said, though he didn't sound overly confident.

"Ayre, head to the landing with Jileli and Lithia. There may be more traps."

He did. Next, the mage and archer carefully crept down the stairs, avoiding the stair Perric was stranded on. When they got there, Saria moved behind Perric.

"Ayre, check the next set of stairs."

"Saria, I don't like this at all," the thief said.

She wasn't sure if he was worried for them, or if it was a blow to his professional ego. She didn't care one way or the other. "Do it."

After a few minutes, the thief announced it was safe.

"There is another landing down about twenty feet. The stairs switchback around in a square. There are two hallways that are collapsed, but the stairs continue."

"Everyone wait at the next landing. Perric will be joining you shortly. Hand me your sword."

"But Saria—" Ayre said.

"Now, Ayre. We need to keep going," Saria said.

"You're the leader." He sulked down the stairs, the light from the globe casting a shadow of his figure on the wall.

Perric handed her his sword over his shoulder. She placed it on the step next to her. Stair traps were notorious finicky. Even with Ayre's skill, there was no guarantee the trap wouldn't spring and kill Perric, Ayre, or both. It wasn't a risk she could take. Unless this was burning oil or the entire stairwell collapsed, what she had in mind was the safest course.

"Saria, just leave—"

Saria sat on the step behind Perric and, with both feet, kicked the paladin square in the lower back, where his armor was the thickest. The big man flew forward and crashed down the stairs like a drunk who'd forgotten how to stand. A scythe swung down, barely missing the paladin as he fell. It embedded in the far wall with a solid *thunk*.

The paladin didn't fare as well. He bounced down the steps and came to a stop on the landing. Saria used his sword to tap the pressure plate, but the trap had been sprung. She ran down and helped Perric to his feet.

The paladin had blood flowing from the side of his mouth. "You could have warned me. I bit my tongue, but other than being a mass of bruises tomorrow, I don't think I broke anything."

She handed him his sword. "It was the only way to get you off the step in one piece. No doubt the designers accounted for someone trying to jump, but not someone getting rudely kicked in the behind."

Perric glared at her. "What if it released poison or fire?"

"Then we'd be dead. Let's keep going."

They joined the others on the next landing. Two hallways led to the left and right, but they were filled to the ceiling with rubble. Whatever had happened to this place in the past century had destroyed a large portion of the temple.

"I checked the next level while you were teaching Perric to fly. The stairs are clear. There is a large room at the base," Ayre said.

"Let's move."

Ayre took the lead, with Perric behind him. The disciples of Insus had devised a lot of measures to protect the orb, if that was the most important thing they were guarding.

The doorway allowed two people to walk through. The room itself was large, though the ceiling wasn't that high. On the left and right sides were six matching statues of scantily clad women holding what looked like wine urns on their shoulders. The walls were covered with murals of Insus and the hunt.

"They certainly liked to kill stuff," Jileli said from behind Saria.

"Yes, they did." The paladin's sword was still dull, so there weren't any undead nearby. "From the look of things, this place has been abandoned for a long time."

"It doesn't matter as long as we find the orb," Ayre said. "I'm going to scout out the room."

"We all go in," Saria said. There was nothing out of place, though in a deserted temple how would you know? Her nerves were on edge after the trap on the stairs. "We stay together."

"Agreed." Lithia entered the room and stood off to the side.

The rest followed her inside while Ayre searched every inch of the floor.

The creepy statue's eyes seem to be following Saria as she walked further into the room. Nothing happened. Ayre had reached the second set of statues when the door behind the Blades slammed down, cutting off their retreat.

"There's probably magic to close the entry door in order to open the far door," Ayre said. "Don't worry about it."

With a loud gurgling sound, a thick black liquid started to pour from the maidens' urns.

"Sure, nothing to worry about," Perric said.

22

Ayre, get that door open," Saria said. "Everyone, get to the far end of the room."

"It's barely a puddle," Ayre said as he strolled to the far door. "Obviously, the trap doesn't work anymore."

The gurgling noise rose in volume until more black tar spewed from the twelve urns the maidens held. The pools grew rapidly as the volume of goo increased.

"Will you shut up!" Perric yelled at Ayre as the team ran to the exit door. "Every time you open your mouth, it gets worse."

"Look here—"

"Ayre," Saria interrupted. "Door first, bitching later."

"Fine." He took his roll of thieves' tools out and selected a pick. He placed a metal shield over the blade and inserted it into the lock. Next, he set a turning tool in the lock and jiggled until the lock clicked. "No worries. The door is unlocked."

"Great, let's get out of here," Lithia said. "I don't like the looks of this."

Small pieces of tile fell from the ceiling to plop into the

viscous black puddle that had spread to cover the area around the statues and was oozing toward the middle.

"Allow me." Ayre turned the door handle and pushed. Nothing moved. He shoved again to the same result. Behind them the goo cascaded and burbled. "The door appears to be stuck."

Saria threw her body into the door, only to bounce off it like it was a brick wall. "I thought you unlocked it?"

"We better get it open soon or we are going to be swimming in this crap," Perric said.

"There are runes around the door." Jileli stepped closer to read them. "They are faint, but they are warding spells. I can try to dispel them, but it will take a few minutes to prepare the ritual."

"What do we do?" Ayre's confidence seemed shaken by the failure to open the door. The ooze sputtered and coughed before resuming a robust flow.

"I need a flat place that will remain clean to set up the spell. If it is disturbed, it won't work."

"Look around," Saria said, walking back into the room, staying out of the ever-increasing goop. The only things in the room were the statues. The tiles from above had sunk into the muck. From the entry door up to a few feet from the exit, the goo crawled along the tile floor. "There has to be a way to shut the goo off. The traps were meant to stop intruders, but the acolytes had to be able to come and go from the temple."

"What is that smell?" Lithia asked as she checked around the statues for anything to help Jileli.

"Sulfur," Saria said. "Oh, fuck. We need to move faster."

"The ooze isn't going to drown us anytime soon," Ayre said. "If anyone lights a candle, we'll be burnt to death instead. If my guess is right from the sulfur smell, the muck is flammable."

As if in response to the thief's comments, the torrent of goo increased.

"Shut up, Ayre," the whole group shouted at him.

"Wait," Saria said. "Ayre, tell it to turn off."

"The ooze will stop," Ayre said.

The urns belched, and the flow spouted like water from a broken dam.

"We were right. Ayre, keep your mouth shut. You are triggering the trap."

"Oh—" Ayre began. The ooze pumped out faster, if that was possible.

"Seriously, do I need to gag you?" Saria asked. "Every time you talk, it gets worse."

The goo now covered the floor and began to deepen at an alarming rate. It the matter of minutes, the syrupy ooze rose, clinging to the top of her boots. "I don't see anywhere clean to do the spell."

Jileli held the components in her hands. "I can't put it on the floor. I can't draw the symbols in liquid."

Lithia fired an arrow into the ceiling. It stuck. "Can we pull that tile out? It would be the right size."

"Ayre, come here. Silently. I'll boost you," Perric said. He clasped his hands together like a stirrup and the thief stepped into it. The big man straightened, and Ayre reached the arrow. He pulled, and the arrow popped loose without freeing the segment. Ayre tossed it back to Lithia before grabbing his dagger. He chipped away at the edges of the tile, showering Perric with dust.

The level of goo continued to rise as the thief fought to loosen the tile. Ayre mimed dusting off his hands as the tile crumbled instead of coming free in one piece.

"Keep trying," Saria said. "Lithia, see if the statues move."

"What if they have traps on them?" the archer asked.

"You think this can get worse?" Saria answered.

"Good point."

Saria sloshed through the syrupy muck to the closest statue and looked it over. It portrayed a human or elvish woman with her hair in a bun and a skirt wrapped around her waist. The urn on her shoulder pointed down and was currently pouring the black sulfur goo into the room. Her eyes faced into the room. Saria took hold of her head and tried to rotate it. It didn't budge. She pulled her foot from the muck with a loud sucking sound and kicked the statue, attempting to break free a piece of the stone that could be used as a makeshift table.

"Any luck?" Lithia asked from the other row of statues.

"Not yet."

Saria tried to pull the arm holding the wrap. Still nothing. She grabbed the urn and tried to tug it. The urn slid forward. "The urn moves."

She rotated it to the left until she heard a sharp crack. "I think I found the trigger to stop the ooze."

"The muck is still pouring out," Lithia said. "My urn doesn't budge."

"Try the next in line. It may take a couple to stop the trap."

The urn almost faced to the left. Just a bit further. Saria pushed on the urn until she heard another crack. The arm holding the urn shattered and the whole thing fell to the floor. Goo sprayed in all directions from the broken stump of an arm.

"We need to find a place for me to cast before it gets much deeper," Jileli called. The goo was mid-calf now and climbing.

"I think I've got it," Ayre yelled. He pulled a large piece of tile free. He held it out, and it crumbled into pieces.

"Ayre, keep a lid on it." Saria eyed the statues nervously to see if they erupted into goo volcanoes, but they remained the same. Was the trap as triggered as it was going to be?

"Fire!" Jileli screamed from the doorway. From above the far door, a globe of fire descended into the room.

Nope. The trap could get worse.

Lithia snatched the bow from her shoulder and shot off an arrow. It struck the globe and pinned it to the wall. "That will buy us a minute or two."

"We are running out of time," Saria said. The muck reached her knees, limiting their movement. If the lock was at the other end of the room, they'd never make it. "Get to the door. We'll have to break it down."

Ayre hopped out of Perric's grip. The thief opened his mouth, and Perric slapped his hand across it. "Every time you speak, it triggers the next part of the trap."

Ayre gestured at the ceiling rudely and then at the statues.

"I'll handle it," Perric said. "Jileli, use my back."

He got on his hands and knees. Most of the paladin vanished into the black ooze.

Jileli wasted no time. She handed the components to Ayre. "Stay behind me while I'm casting."

Saria and Lithia slogged through the ooze. Each step became more difficult as the levels continued to rise. They finally reached the group. The fire Lithia had pinned to the wall sparked and sputtered, casting embers down. When the liquid reached a high enough level, the sparks would ignite the room and burn them all to death.

Jileli uncorked a vial and drew a circle on Perric's scale mail armor. While not perfect, the circle clung together. She pulled the next vial and created glyphs around the outside of the circle.

The ooze was creeping up to Perric's chest. He lifted his head to keep his face out of the muck.

"Don't move," Jileli said. "I'm almost done."

"Hopefully, he doesn't drown in this stuff," Lithia said.

Saria hoped the same, but putting more pressure on the mage didn't seem like a great idea.

Jileli moved like a huckster sliding pieces around in a shell game. When everything was done, she cut her arm and dropped her blood into the middle of the circle.

Light flared from the circle. The doorway glowed with a deep purple color that ran to black where it crossed the etched runes. One by one, the runes vanished and the door unlatched.

"It's done," Jileli said, pulling Perric up before the ooze forced itself into the big man's nose and mouth.

A loud rumbling came from below them.

"What now?" Ayre said.

"Ayre!"

"Get out the door," Saria said, pushing the others closer.

Lithia grabbed the handle and tugged. The door didn't budge against the weight of the goo. "It's still stuck."

"Wait," Jileli said. "The urn stopped."

The rumbling continued for a moment before a loud sucking noise filled the room. The ooze was receding. After a few moments, a grate in the floor could be seen where the ooze was returning to its reservoir. Lithia pulled the door open, releasing some of the goo into the next room, but the Blades were more than happy to escape. Saria shoved the door closed behind them.

They all collapsed on the floor of the empty hallway.

"Well, that was fun," Ayre said in his usual sarcastic tone.

Saria sighed. "I told you your mouth would get us killed one day."

23

Saria started at the sounds of scraping. Ayre had a large jar out and was scooping the muck from the death trap into it. The thief had a grin on his face.

"What are you doing?" Saria asked.

Ayre lifted his jar as if toasting her. "This goo has been waiting underground for who knows how long without drying up or anything. If it could be reproduced by an alchemist, we could make a fortune."

"We could have all been fried, and you are concerned with gold?" Lithia's face reflected the irritation she felt.

"But we didn't die, and gold is good."

"I think I know what happened," Jileli said from where she slumped on the floor with her back against the wall. "The trap magically attached itself to the first person who spoke in the room. There probably is a code phrase to turn it off, and Ayre didn't know it."

"That makes as much sense as anything else about this place." Saria used the backside of her dagger to scrape as much muck off her boots and pants as possible. Poor Perric. The man was covered with the black ooze.

"See," Ayre said with a huff. "It wasn't my fault."

"No, it was," Perric said from where he was trying to clean his sword on an old rag. "If you had kept your mouth shut, we could have avoided the ooze all together."

Ayre rose to his feet. "I'm going to scout ahead while you all blame me for everything."

Saria started to say something, but Perric shook his head.

Ayre pulled his dagger and stalked along the hall. He was being far more diligent in searching for traps than normal. A few minutes later, he turned a corner, and the hallway went dark again.

Perric threw the ruined cloth on the floor and dropped down next to Saria. "He's always slid by on his wits, but he's never run into a situation like this, and it has shaken his confidence. He'll be fine, but he needs to learn there is more to being a Blade than collecting loot."

Lithia joined them on the ground. "I know the type. Ayre is a legend in his own mind, so I'm sure this is tough on him. My last team had a mage with a similar disposition, but he didn't have skill Ayre does, and he died when a spell backfired on him."

"I've known him for a few years, but this bounty is far more difficult than any we've faced before. I'm not sure if we can get out of here intact," Saria said, noticing Jileli had curled up on the floor and was napping. Magic took a toll on all mages and that last spell must have been powerful, but it had saved their asses.

"We should have stayed in Moonbourne," Perric said, leaning back against the wall.

The big man looked tired, and they'd been in the temple for over half a day by Saria's timekeeping. Without any way to see the sky, she didn't know if it had been four hours or days. Time became meaningless underground. "Grab a few minutes of rest. I'll keep watch for Ayre."

"I don't think you need to worry," Lithia said with a low chuckle. She nodded toward Perric.

The big man's head was against the wall, and he was sound asleep. "Well, you get some rest as well."

Lithia nodded, headed back toward the door, and laid down. She was softly snoring almost immediately.

Maybe they'd been in here for longer than she realized. Saria felt tired, but not exhausted. The others were out. Knowing Ayre's frustration, he'd push himself to keep going long past exhaustion. He'd need to rest before they explored the next part of the temple.

On one hand, she agreed with Perric. They should have stayed in Moonbourne and not taken this bounty. Why had Brar Opalback wanted the Blades for this mission besides the fact she knew Saria? That was a question she'd been mulling over the whole time and still had no clue. If obtaining the orb was the most crucial thing, Regina could have recommended bands that were far stronger and more experienced. Like Chaos Clan—who was now missing.

The obvious answer was that Regina was the one who trusted her, not Brar. But why tell her Brar was the one who'd asked for her?

She would insist on the answers to these questions when they returned with the orb, especially now that assassins were involved. She was going to have to talk to Regina about the death markers and the Skulls and Talos, anyway.

Ayre sulked back down the hall. "There is a huge room a couple hundred feet down the hallway."

"Grab some sleep and then we'll go explore."

He nodded. "You know I would never endanger the team, right?"

"Ayre, I trust you with my life. Not with my sister or my gold, but I do with my life."

He smiled at her. "Wise woman."

He found some empty floor near Lithia and was asleep in a few minutes.

What would they face next trying to find the orb? Whatever it was, it wouldn't be good.

A few hours later, everyone was fed, rested, and ready to go. "How long have we been in here?" Lithia asked while stretching her arms and legs.

"My best guess is about a day," Saria said, getting her sword out.

"We may be in here for days" Ayre spun a dagger in his fingers while he waited for the group to set out. "There is no way to know how big this place is."

"Let's just hope the orb isn't trapped behind one of the collapsed sections," Saria said. "I really don't want to have to dig our way to it."

"Agreed." Perric's sword was still normal, so at least they were away from the undead.

"Let's get going," Saria said. "Ayre in front. Perric, protect the back."

"Got it," Perric said.

"Shall we?" Ayre said with a sweeping bow.

Saria laughed. More from nerves than anything else. The place was getting to her. "I'm sleeping outside for a week after this one."

Ayre set out at a good clip. Since he'd scouted earlier, Saria was reasonably sure there weren't any traps in the hall. The main hallway ran fifty feet before turning to the left. They passed three halls that were all collapsed.

"Every collapsed hall we pass increases the chances the orb is down one of them," Lithia said, pointing at the third mound of rubble blocking a passageway. "If it is, I'm going to scream."

"We all will." Jileli had recovered from her earlier fatigue, though she still looked tired. Saria slowed down to walk next to her.

"Do you need more rest?" Saria studied the mage's face for a moment. "We have no idea what's up ahead, and we may need your magic to get us through."

"I'm fine." Jileli walked for a few moments, seemingly distracted. "Blood magic demands a lot from the practitioner. Being half-succubus makes me far stronger than a human would be, but also takes more out of me. The last spell was complex, and it drained me, but sleep and my elixir helped restore my energy. I'll be out for a week after we return to Moonbourne."

Everyone had their weaknesses. The Blades would need to take Jileli's quirks into account, the same as they would other members, so the more she learned about the blood mage, the better. "So you can do different types of magic? Is that typical?"

Jileli smiled ruefully. "It is when you have two different ancestries that can do different magic."

Saria couldn't think of a graceful way to ask if people new to demon magic could feel it pull at them, so she just said, "If you need rest, tell me. I can't afford to have you collapse in the middle of a fight."

"I will," Jileli said with a smirk. "Somebody has to keep Ayre in line."

"I heard that," Ayre said, eliciting laughs from the group.

The hallway took two more turns, passing even more collapsed tunnels. Each time they found another one, the mood sank.

After a left turn, Saria swore there was light up ahead. The closer they got, the more she believed it. Could it be daylight? Undead hated fire, so she doubted it was torches. She halted the group, "Ayre, what's up there?"

The thief went ahead and soon returned to the group. "I didn't go in, but there is a glow from the room. From the doorway, it looks like a throne room."

"A throne in a temple seems odd," Perric said. "I've been in many temples to Drohara and never seen a throne room. Maybe a prayer room?"

"Could be," Ayre said with a shrug. "I tend to avoid holy places."

"Smart move," Perric said.

Ayre glared at him but said nothing.

"Let's go in," Saria said. "As long as there are no statues holding urns anywhere."

Ayre entered the room through the archway with Saria on his heels. She had her sword out. The glow stone in her left hand prevented her from using her dirk, but it was better than fumbling around in the dark. When she confirmed there was enough light to see by from all the torches along the walls, she stored the stone and pulled her knife free.

A large room spread out before them. It was thirty feet wide and forty feet long. The walls held vividly colored murals of Insus's great hunts. Men, women, and all sorts of animals and monsters were immortalized on the walls and ceiling. At the far end of the room, a curved, raised dais came out of the center of the back wall. On top sat an immense throne with a lifeless body in it. A headdress rested on its bony head, and its robes were tattered and discolored with age. A staff with a glowing orb leaned against the right armrest. From a distance, it looked like the orb in the drawing.

Lithia fired an arrow at the corpse. It hit the body with a resounding thud, but nothing else happened. "It must be dead?"

"Let's hope so." Perric's sword was not glowing, which meant the corpse wasn't a zombie waiting around for someone to bite. "I've had my fill of undead."

Saria stepped forward, but Ayre grabbed her arm. A ten by ten portion of the floor dropped out from where she had stepped. "It's trapped."

"Thank you, Ayre." Saria peered into a darkened pit that was deeper than she expected. The construction work that must have gone into creating this maze was unbelievable. Whoever built this place was intent on guarding its treasures.

"Be careful," the thief said, studying the floor. "It looks like there are more scattered across the room."

"Ayre, we need to get to the throne. Best guess, that's the orb on the staff."

The thief's eyes lit up. "Time to finish this bounty and get the fuck out of here."

"You said it." Jileli carried her component pouch in her left hand.

"Ready?" Ayre asked.

Before they could answer, a low chuckle filled the room. The figure's head straightened, and its eyes glowed red. The flesh was desiccated, showing all the bones beneath the parchment-thin skin. It had long white hair, wore long red robes, and its eyes glowed a deep red. It pushed itself up to stand. "I am Hesic, high priest of Insus. I welcome you all to my chambers. Please make yourself at home. You won't be leaving. Ever."

24

Not a zombie. A lich. The sneaky mother fucker. Saria would rather fight a herd of zombies than a lich.

Perric stepped forward, his winged sword bursting into golden light, flooding the room with its brilliance. "We are here to retrieve the ashen orb. Give it to us and you may return to your slumber unharmed. In the name of Drohara, I swear it to be true."

"The goddess of light has no sway in the domain of Insus. By violating the treaty amongst the gods, you have relinquished your right to life. You will replace my guards as the price for destroying them." Hesic hefted his staff. The orb swirled with darkness.

"Yet we overcame your traps and your fighters. We will take the orb." Perric's sword seem to intensify with each word.

"Lord Insus bade me to protect the orb for all eternity. The mortal realm is not equipped to deal with the ashen orb's magic. You would destroy the world in search of gold?" Hesic asked.

On Saria's signal, Ayre and Lithia moved to opposite sides of the room. Saria and Jileli flanked Perric who stood just shy of the pit. "We will not yield to the undead. You are an abomination, and I shall destroy you as the light does the darkness."

The lich began to clap. "What a fine speech, mighty paladin. Shall we see if your proficiency with arms matches your ability to bore me?"

Perric brought his sword up in front of him. It glowed like the noon sun.

Hesic stabbed his staff toward Perric. A black bolt streaked across the room. At the last instant, Perric swung his sword, striking the bolt and sending it into the wall in front of Lithia.

Flames burst from the impact site, throwing chucks of rock and fire across the left side of the room. A piece of stone clipped Lithia on the side of the head, dropping her to the floor. The archer pushed herself to her hands and knees before vomiting all over the place.

Saria started to run to her side, but Lithia waved her off. "I'm fine. Kill that thing."

Hesic started down the stairs, firing more black bolts as he went.

Ayre dove back, barely avoiding a missile. He covered his head as rocks flew across the room. He rolled to his feet, grabbed a stone, and threw it across the floor.

"Not much of a shot, are you, elf?"

A trap door fell open a few feet in front of Perric. Ayre smiled. "It depends on what you're aiming at."

Hesic swung his staff in front of him. A wave of magic rippled down the center of the room.

The spell struck Perric, Jileli, and Saria before they could react. Jileli grabbed her head and screamed, going to her knees.

Saria stood transfixed. Her mind screamed to run. Her training kept her body held in place. Fear swarmed her thoughts like insects swarming a piece of bread. She struggled to free herself, but the terrifying images flashing through mind refused to release her.

Perric trudged forward hesitantly.

Images of her companions dying in horrible ways flooded Saria's brain, but she rose through the terror to regain control.

Perric couldn't do this alone. None of them could. She would ignore these fears for her team.

Vision clearing, Saria assessed the room. Ayre had opened one of the traps, but how many more were there? They would need to fight the lich and avoid the traps in the floor at the same time.

Another stone flew off to Perric's right. The trap door fell open, showing the path through.

Perric ran closer to the lich.

Jileli continued to scream in terror. The mage sobbed, hugging herself tightly and rocking back and forth like a child. The lich's fear spell tried to snag Saria again, and she fisted her hands around the hilts of her weapons.

"I am stronger than this," Saria said. The last of the fear dissipated. How close were the others to shaking it off? Lithia still was down. The fire continued to burn all around her. Perric couldn't reach the lich without risking more traps. Ayre, who apparently had shaken off the spell effortlessly, danced around a barrage of missiles as Hesic tried to eliminate him.

Saria knelt in front of Jileli and shook her. The mage whimpered and sobbed, unaware of Saria's presence.

"We need Jileli!" Perric knocked another bolt onto the floor. The force of the blow shook the room and two more trap doors dropped.

"I'm sorry," Saria said before slapping the mage across the face.

Jileli's head jerked up. "What happened?"

"Fear magic. Perric needs help."

Jileli stood. Her eyes flared and her horns glowed purple. She pulled a vial from her pouch, poured the green liquid into her palm, and shouted something in the language she used for magic, one that grew increasingly familiar to Saria each time Jileli cast spells.

A low fog rolled away from the mage. It slithered like a snake across the floor toward Hesic.

The lich gestured, and the fog vanished like it had never been.

"Ayre, am I clear?" Perric asked.

Two stones flew over the paladin's head, releasing a door between him and the lich. "Go!"

Perric ran toward the lich. He swung his sword at the lich's head. Hesic blocked the blow, though the force drove him back.

Avoiding the trap doors, Saria sped into the fight. She slid to the right and jabbed her sword at the exposed flank of their enemy. Before her blade sliced into him, he vanished.

"Where did he go?" Saria pushed her back against Perric and swung her sword in a pattern in front of her. Perric did the same. Invisible enemies were the worst, but they'd fought worse.

"Oh, no, you don't," Jileli said as she threw a glob of red into the air over her head. The substance paused before breaking into thousands of balls. They flew across the room and struck the invisible lich where he'd moved on the dais. As the onslaught continued, the form of Hesic emerged.

Apparently, the beads did more than reveal the invisible undead. They caused him pain. The lich hissed and flinched each time he was struck.

"You can hide shit, but you can still smell it, lich boy." Ayre threw a knife at the lich's writhing form. It struck it in the chest, but the struggle continued. Perric charged at the lich, sword raised.

Hesic swung his staff, striking Perric in the chest. A burst of dark energy, along with a shock wave, threw the paladin across the room like a ragdoll. He crashed to the stone floor before sliding into one of the open pits.

"Perric!" Saria screamed. Ayre grabbed her arm, preventing her from hurling herself to where she'd last seen the paladin.

"He'll kill us if you stop to help Perric. He may already be dead," Ayre said. His words were harsh, but he was right.

Saria channeled her rage into her body and ran toward the lich. He threw more of the black bolts at Saria but she dodged them and struck a vicious upper cut. The sword carved a groove through Hesic's robe, but nothing else happened.

Well, except for the lich nearly taking her head off. Hesic swung his staff at her before she could return to a defensive position, but Ayre stopped the blow between his crossed knives. He kicked the lich in the knee, knocking the undead priest to the floor. He swung his knife in an overhand blow to embed it between the lich's eyes.

Faster than a serpent, the lich rolled aside and drove his staff into Ayre's chest. It threw the thief back to slam on the floor. His leather satchel tore open, throwing his belongings all over the place. The thief slid across the tiles toward an open trapdoor, but the strap caught on a piece of broken stone. It stopped Ayre before he met the same fate as Perric.

"Enough," Jileli yelled. She'd drawn a spell out on the floor. "Begone, lich!"

She touched the circle, allowing her magic to flow into it.

Mist rose, coalescing as it grew. Anxiety shuddered inside Saria as this spell pulled at her and threatened to mesmerize her in the middle of battle.

A form began to take shape. "You summoned me, mistress?"

A gray figure stepped from the fog. It stood about three feet tall, had horns and lots of teeth. Its eyes glowed red, and the room smelled of brimstone within a second.

"Ixipopix, kill the lich."

The demon grinned, showing a wider array of teeth. "Of course, mistress. May I eat the elf after?"

"No, he is under my protection, as are all the others. Kill the lich."

The demon jumped across the room in a single bound, landing on Hesic. The demon's talons tore chunks of dead flesh from the lich's body. Its teeth sunk into the undead's shoulder and held on.

Saria took the opportunity to drive her sword into Hesic's side.

Hesic screamed.

The sword stuck in the lich's body like an ax in a tree. She pulled, but it didn't budge. Unfortunately, this put her within Hesic's reach, and he backhanded her with a lot more power than a bag of bones ought to have.

The blow felt like a sledgehammer, sending her across the room. If she landed in a pit... But she didn't. Her breath whooshed out of her body when she smacked into the floor. She scrambled to find a hand hold to stop her momentum. She bumped into Ayre.

Saria sat up in time to see an arrow slam into the side of the lich's head. The demon tore at the lich, who fought back desperately.

Ayre groaned. The elf had a gash across his forehead and

147

blood running down his face. He was moving, which was a good sign.

The lich screamed a guttural word, and the room stilled. The demon was yanked away from Hesic as if by an invisible hand. With a ripping noise, the demon fractured into two parts and dissolved into mist.

Jileli collapsed.

"Now, I will make you suffer for this travesty," Hesic said as he bore down on Saria. "You will wish your parents had kept you in the crèche."

Saria reached for her dirk, but she'd lost it when the lich had hit her. She scanned around for a weapon, any weapon, to use against the lich.

"You will suffer for all eternity for what you've done to me." Hesic stormed toward her since she was the closest one of their group who was conscious. The only other member still standing was Lithia, over by the far wall.

Ayre's lockpicking kit and other of the thief's possessions were scattered around Saria. None were useful. Small sacks of coins, a few gems, a bracelet, and the bottle of goo from the trap. The probably flammable goo.

She grabbed the bottle. "Lithia, shoot a fire arrow at this bastard."

The archer grabbed a padded arrow from her quiver and stuck it into the fire burning near her. She nocked the arrow, took careful aim, and held it.

Saria reared back and threw the jar at Hesic. It shattered, sending the ooze over the lich's clothes. "Now!"

Lithia let loose, and the arrow struck Hesic in the chest. Instantly he burst into flames, lit up like a bonfire. The lich threw himself to the floor, but the fire, fueled by the ooze, ignited the centuries-old material. And the centuries-old body.

"No! Eternals be damned, I—"

The lich collapsed like a deflating balloon, leaving a puddle of flame on the stone floor. The staff fell, shattering the orb.

Saria thought she would cry.

25

Saria stared at the broken glass of the ashen orb. All of the things they'd gone through just to lose the prize at the last second. But she would give up any artifact, any bounty in the world, to have saved Perric from that pit.

"You'd think a magical artifact could take one drop on the floor," Ayre said, sitting behind Saria. He glanced around. "What happened? I hit my head pretty hard."

A loud clang came from behind them. A mailed hand emerged from the trap.

"Perric!" Saria scrambled to her feet and ran to where the paladin was climbing out. The big man had his left hand wedged between the door mechanism and the floor.

"It's about time," Perric said.

"Let's get you out of there." She grabbed his hand and assisted the scrambling Perric out of the pit. His face was red from exertion as he finally cleared the edge.

He put his hands on his knees, catching his breath. "Damn, I thought I was a destined for Drohara's realm for a minute."

"How did you not fall?" Saria asked. The big man had gone over the edge pretty quickly.

"I grabbed for the edge and missed, but my gauntlet caught between the floor and the door. It stopped me long enough to get a grasp. I called, but the fight was too loud."

Relief rushed through her and threatened to spout out of her eyes as tears. No time for that "Sorry," she said gruffly. "Hesic was a tough old bastard. We barely finished him."

"It was a close call for sure." Perric stepped over to the pit and held his hand out. He muttered words under his breath, and a couple moments later, his sword streaked up out of the pit to rest in his hand.

"Nice trick," Lithia said as she approached. The archer sported a darkening bruise on the side of her face, and blood streaked her jerkin.

"Good shot at the end." Saria took a seat next to the befuddled Ayre.

"I'm glad to see everyone is still in one piece." Jileli had dark circles under her eyes. She slumped down next to Saria.

"What was that…" Lithia began, her hand moving as if she was searching for a word. "Stuff you threw at the lich?"

"Ayre's gold mine ooze," Saria said with a chuckle. She glanced at Ayre to see his reaction to using the prize he'd wanted to sell, but he just stared off into the void.

Perric sheathed his sword and knelt in front of the thief. He pulled Ayre into a seated position, then placed his hands on either side of his head and intoned a prayer of healing. The paladin's hands glowed golden as the spell released.

"Perric, I love you like a brother, but why are you holding my head? I know it's been a few days. I'll stab you if you try to kiss me," Ayre said, a wry smile on his face.

"You could have left him for a bit longer," Saria said with a grin. "I was enjoying the quiet."

"Seriously, what happened?" Ayre asked, his eyes going over the room. "Where is the orb?"

"It broke," Lithia said. "The staff hit the ground, and it shattered."

"Magical artifacts are normally much stronger," Ayre said.

Saria chuckled. "You already said that."

"I did?"

"Yes. Let's take a few hours to rest then we can regroup," Saria said. The fight had taken a lot out of all of them. "This room should be safe enough for now, as long as you avoid the pits."

"I'll take the watch," Perric said.

Saria didn't argue and was out as soon as her head hit the floor.

"Based on my guess, the lich wasn't using the ashen orb, but he was guarding it, so it stands to reason it is here, somewhere," Ayre said. The thief had gathered the pieces of the broken artifact and claimed they were not the same material as pre-war artifacts tended to be.

Saria chewed on her rations while she listened to the thief. She hoped they'd faced the worst the temple had to offer. What could be worse than a lich? She stopped that train of thought. If there was something, she didn't want to know.

"I'm going to search the dais, while you all look over the walls for clues," Ayre said. "Stay out of the center of the room. I think I opened all the traps, but who knows in this place. Questions?"

"No," Lithia said, pushing herself up. "I'm ready for a hot meal and a warm bed. Let's find the orb."

They all got up. Ayre climbed the stairs and began

searching the throne. The others each took a wall. The detail on the murals amazed Saria. They were so intricate that if the beasts stepped out and became real, she wouldn't have been surprised.

The search went on for a while. Ayre broke the silence. "Nothing of any use up here. Has anyone found anything interesting?"

"There is magical residue on the walls, probably from the spell that illuminates the room, but it is stronger over here," Jileli said from where she searched on the right wall.

Ayre walked to where she was. He studied the area for a bit. His hands traced the image of a hydra that Insus fought. With a sharp click, an oddly shaped door about as tall as the elf opened. The outline must be part of camouflaging the door "Ahh, there you are."

"Good find, Jileli," Perric said as the team assembled at the hidden door.

"Thank you." The mage's shy smile was one they hadn't seen often since she'd joined the Blades. This bounty mission had been a true test of their two newest members, for certain.

"Ayre, is it clear?" Saria asked.

The thief examined the door jamb, carefully checking every inch and bump. "No, it's clear. It looks like it is a natural fissure, not built."

"Interesting." Saria peered over Ayre's shoulder into the fissure that led, as everything in this temple, into the darkness. The pale sandy walls gleamed in the light of the light stones. "Ayre, lead the way. Perric, bring up the rear," Saria said, and they set off.

The path was narrow enough that Perric scraped the walls in a couple of the closer parts. Without the glow stones, they would have never been able to follow the twisting natural corridor. Even Jileli, by far the smallest and slightest of the Blades, had to duck to get through the lower parts. The stone held a glistening ore in it that reflected the light. It would have been beautiful if Saria wasn't so concerned about what they were walking into.

"We've arrived," Ayre said as the fissure opened into a huge cave. The floor was covered with pools of stagnant water.

The stench made Saria want to lose her earlier meal, but she forced it down. She saw nothing that could be causing the odor besides the water—no piles of bodies, no slime or fungi, no more undead.

"I guess they haven't cleaned up in a while," Ayre said.

"Less talking. Let's find the orb and get to some fresh air," Jileli said. The mage had a cloth over her face.

A raised stone walkway led to a platform in the center of the cavern. From the far end of the room, light filtered in through what looked like an exit. The faint crash of waves could be heard in the stillness. Two rings were carved into the stone, with runes at the ordinal points of the circle. Stone pillars about three feet high were placed at each of those points. A compass had been scribed inside the circles. Light shimmered across the area. In the center circle sat a pedestal with a glowing orb on top.

"There she is," Ayre whispered from the edge of the circle.

All of this just to get an artifact for a sorceress who we have no idea what she'll use it for. Between the Skull Posse, the undead, traps, and the fucking lich, what else could this bounty throw at them? Probably better not to ask. It was time to snatch the orb and get out of here with everyone intact.

Saria stepped next to Ayre and marveled at the sight. White tiles the size of Saria's hand were laid out on the ground before them as if someone had set up a game then left. "Is it safe?"

"Probably not, but we made it this far," Perric said from behind Saria. "What do we do now?"

"Ayre, can you spot any traps? Jileli, do you recognize the glyphs?" Saria asked.

"They are the basic symbols of magic." Jileli moved closer without crossing the outer ring. "It's a spell of sorts."

"What kind of spell?" Lithia had her bow out and fidgeted with the bowstring.

"I'm not sure." Jileli studied the closest rune before she added, "These are just set there. They aren't part of the floor."

"I don't see anything unusual." Ayre put his hand out to cross the outer ring. Nothing happened. "Well, we can take the glyphs. I have a feeling they'll fit into the slots in the pillars."

The mage reached out and retrieved a rune. She flipped it over. "There are runes on the back as well."

Ayre tried to step across the inner ring but couldn't. An angry red light flared from where his foot touched the inner circle. "Protective spell. They didn't take any chances."

"Collect the tiles," Jileli said. "I have an idea."

Ayre retrieved the three remaining rune tiles and handed them to the mage. She laid them out on the floor in front of her. Under each, she drew the corresponding letter in the dust. Next she flipped over each tile and added those the letters to the list. H, T, E, M, P, Y, O, N were scrawled in the dirt.

"I think that the runes act as the key to the orb. We just need to create the right word," Jileli said.

"You can spell HOME," Lithia said, watching over the mage's shoulder.

"You can spell THEM," Saria suggested.

"You can also spell PHYN, which translates to god in the Eldar language," Ayre said. The thief spun his dagger between his fingers.

"Let's try HOME," Perric said. "It could be that the orb is going home."

"As good a guess as any," Ayre said. Jileli handed the thief the tiles in order. He quickly went to each pillar and set one tile into the slot on the top, going clockwise from the north position. When he set the last tile, nothing happened.

"Try THEM," Saria said. They repeated the trial without success for each word. Ayre handed the mage all of the tiles to lay them out again.

"OPEN," Jileli said with a laugh. "It spells open."

"Could it be that simple?" Perric asked.

"Why not?" Ayre said. "It makes sense and is easy to remember."

"Wait," Jileli said as she picked up the O tile to hand to Ayre. "There is a small mark at the base. The rune translates to EA, but the meaning is oneness. I think we have to set them down at the same time."

"It's worth a try," Saria said. Ayre handed each of them a tile while Jileli stayed where she was. Each took their position around the circle. "Ready?"

Once everyone indicated they were, Jileli called, "One, two, three."

Each of the Blades set their tile in place.

That was when the shaking started.

26

Tremors ran through the cavern, sending a flurry of screeching bats headed for the exit on the far side of the room. The shell that protected the orb flashed red three times before it faded from view. Saria stepped into the circle.

"Looks like we did it," Saria said. "Great work, Jileli. Is the earthquake something we need to worry about?"

"It was a very old spell protecting the orb and animating all the zombies, the guards, and the lich." Jileli waved a hand. "I'm not surprised there are aftereffects."

Saria nodded. "Still, we shouldn't hang around here to find out."

The team met up at the pedestal while Ayre checked it. "It's clean."

The orb swirled with a bright blue pattern. The ornate platinum base clearly showed the script that the drawing hadn't. Saria reached over and plucked the orb from its resting place. She pulled a small leather pouch out and placed the orb in it before adding it to her rucksack.

"The bats were nice enough to show us the exit," Lithia said into the silence of the room. "I would like to see the sun."

"Wouldn't we all," Saria said. "Ayre, lead the way."

Ayre stopped at the bottom of a narrow fissure with a steep slope. It was obvious the bats were using this exit a lot from the amount of guano covering the stones and straggly weeds that grew in patches.

"You going to collect all this?" Perric asked the thief.

"If only," Ayre signed. "We would all be rich."

"Enough chatting, I want to see the sun," Saria said.

After a brief but disgusting climb through bat guano, they emerged into an overcast day. Stairs were carved into the side of the rocks leading down to the remains of an old wooden pier. They stared out across the Endless Sea. A strip of sand and dunes followed the shoreline.

"Looks like we walk from here," Perric said. "We are two days north of Tolle. We should be able to get a ship up the Serpent River from there."

"No," Ayre said. "We should cut inland and get a boat from a small town. We don't know if the other bands are still searching Tolle for the missing dagger. We don't need any more run-ins."

Saria considered both options. Either way, it would take a week to get back to Moonbourne. "We do it Ayre's way. First off, let's build a small fire and get some rest. We leave at daybreak."

The team set to building a makeshift camp. After a bit, they had a small fire going with driftwood they gathered from the dunes. Saria sat enjoying the fire, chatting with the team as the sun set and darkness fell. Everyone seemed to have forgiven her for doing as Regina asked and not telling them the whole truth until it was necessary, and Perric hadn't been rude to Jileli in hours. Were things finally looking up?

"I'll take the first watch," Saria said. The others found a comfortable spot in the sand and went to sleep.

Once all was quiet, Saria, with her back to the group, pulled the orb from the leather pouch. It swirled the same brilliant blue as before. What did this do that was worth so much to the sorceress? Would it be better to hand it over or just drop it to the bottom of the Endless Sea where it would never be found?

Professional pride won out. She would give it to Regina and collect the gold they'd been promised. The Blades would be well off, not rich enough to walk away, but comfortable for a while. She returned the orb to its new home and watched over her band while they slept.

ACKNOWLEDGMENTS

Acknowledgement

You are holding in your hand the ninth title I've written to date. I'm not sure how that is possible. In 2017 I sold my first book to Falstaff books under a three-book series contract. Honestly, I didn't have any idea if I could write three books, given it took seven years to complete *Storm Forged*. The thing I found is that once you complete a novel, knowing you can makes the rest easier. Don't get me wrong, it is still a ton of work, but knowing you've done it once is a great comfort when you get stuck.

The Ashen Orb Bounty kicks off a three-novella series set in the world of the Shadow Blades. The next two books, *The Dragon's Wrath Bounty*, and *The Wayward Mage Bounty*, follow our band of adventures on an action-packed quest. The good news is they are already written, so no long waits until the next part of the saga. I may stay with the novella length for the rest of the series or may move to novels after this. I haven't decided yet. I like the shorter format since it lends itself well to the bounty system, but I can also see grouping the connected adventures into a single novel. Time will tell.

2023 has been an awful year for me on a personal level. I lost my best friend to cancer (FUCK CANCER BTW) way to soon. I met Mike in 9th grade in homeroom. He was reading a gaming magazine that came with a cardboard game in the center. It was 1980 so there weren't a lot of other options. I was a D&D player and DM, but Mike was an avid reader, having moved around the world with his military family, and loved board games. We played the latest cardboard games in homeroom and at lunch every day. As we got older, and could drive, we were a fixture at each other's houses to play games with a group of friends. Over the years, he would come visit and we'd play games, and when I married Hope in 2017, he came to the wedding. Once a year he'd spend a week at our house playing games non-stop. We emailed Civ 4 turns back and forth every day. Christmas 2022, he stopped emailing me, and I figured he was busy. After a few days, I called him, and he thought he had COVID. Turns out he had a brain tumor. In February, he was gone.

Later the same year, my friend Sam Lethcoe lost his fight with cancer. He'd been my friend and accountant for over twenty years. Have I mentioned FUCK CANCER?

Through all of this, I'd escape into the world of Providence where the Shadow Blades is set. Writing about Saria and the team kept me sane. When everything else was too much to handle, I could channel my feelings into my fictional family, and it would help ease my sadness. My family, who are amazing, made sure I ate and took breaks, but I think they all knew I needed the time to process.

While things will never be the same, it has gotten easier.

Now that I've dragged you through my personal life, let's get back to the book at hand.

Two of my favorite franchises are *The Witcher* and *Cowboy Bebop*. I thought it would be fun to set a group of bounty hunters in a sword and sorcery world, and I think it was successful. If you agree, leave a review (shameless plug).

A very special thanks to Regina Kirby who won a charity auction to be tuckerized in this book. She is an amazing friend, and what started off as a bit player ended up becoming a major character in the Shadow Blades world. The auction was two parts. First you could have your name used in *The Ashen Orb Bounty* and the second was whether that character lived or died. She ended up winning both sections, so she got the choice to live on. For all of you that were bidding to kill her off in the book, shame on you.

Jody Wallace is my editor on my books I publish through Distracted Dragon Press. She is AMAZING. While my manuscripts have gotten much cleaner over the years, Jody finds all the inconsistencies, plot holes, and missing internal thoughts (so many internal thoughts) so that you have a much more enjoyable read. If you laughed at the Bon Jovi riff, that was for Jody. Emily Leverett did the copy/proof reading on the book. She cleaned up the grammar, killed the typos, and made sure the book was of professional quality. There are always typos, but after so many rounds of edits, they've earned their place in the book if they survived this long.

Natania Barron did the cover which is amazing. She is a fabulous author as well, so you can check out her work on Amazon. John Hartness did the formatting which makes it look like a million bucks. Davey Beauchamp does the chapter header art. He was the cover designer on the Darkest Storm trilogy, and we've been friends ever since.

My family are always my biggest supports of my career. Emily's gamer tag inspired the Eylnian Empire in this series. Nicholas' D&D exploits gave me a couple great ideas that were super fun in the book. Blaze, our dog, wanted the book to be about him in the lands of the pink poodles, but that's another story. My wife Hope is wonderful. She puts up with me burning long hours at night writing these books. She is my alpha reader and sounding board when I'm stuck. She is also the most fabulous wife I could ever hope for. I'd truly be lost without her.

And lastly, thank you for buying and reading my books. I

have dreamed of being an author for as long as I can remember. Without you, these worlds are empty and unneeded.

Until the next book,

Patrick
July 2023

ABOUT THE AUTHOR

Patrick is the author of the award-winning Darkest Storm Series published by Falstaff Books. Other titles include Never Steal From Dragons and Watchers of Astaria series from Distracted Dragon Press. Other publications include Fairy Films: Wee Folk on the Big Screen, a collection of fairy essays. Patrick is a member of SFWA.

An avid gadget user, Patrick is also the Director of Technology Services for Author's Essentials LLC providing solutions and advice for writing professionals. Patrick writings delve into software, hardware, social media, and all things web-related. The primary focus of Author's Essentials is how and when to employ technology to enhance your writing process.

Patrick resides in Charlotte, NC with his wife and two children. In his spare time, he's a PC gamer, homebrewer, 3D printer enthusiast, and DIYer. You can usually find him in the Hearthstone Tavern or wandering Azeroth as a Blood Elf Warlock in the evenings.

You can find out more at https://linktr.ee/patrickdugan

ALSO BY PATRICK DUGAN

The Shadow Blade Series

The Ashen Orb Bounty

The Dragon's Wrath Bounty

The Wayward Mage Bounty

Pixiepunk Series

Never Steal from Dragons

Watchers of Astaria Series

Fate & Flux – Prequel

Of Cogs & Conjuring

Pistols & Potions

Machines & Monsters

The Darkest Storm Series

Storm Forged

Unbreakable Storm

Storm Shattered

www.ingramcontent.com/pod-product-compliance
Lightning Source LLC
Chambersburg PA
CBHW022125170626
46808CB00002B/838